Nicole a Levi —
Wel...
cheers, Nicole

Civil
Dusk

by

Nicole R. Ordway

HCS
HATTON CROSS STEAMPUNK
PUBLISHING

First Edition

Copyright © 2019 Nicole R. Ordway

Edited by Jeanne L. Wilkins

Cover Aurora Imagery by Ann Dinsmore

HCS Publishing

www.hcspublishing.com

All rights reserved.

ISBN: 978-0-578-48504-1

civil dusk – n. The time of evening when the sun is six degrees below the horizon, when the light is still enough for you to see things…and for things to see you.

CHAPTER ONE

The sun's last blaze of glorious rays branched out over the floundering boat and across the rollicking ocean. Hugh could almost hear the celestial orb wailing for salvation - or that might have been the wind kicking up over the deck rails. Unlike the sunrises on the other side of the island, the western waters' sunsets had a harsh character. Brisk and cold and with sunlight jagged like the gnarled twigs of a thousand-year-old lightning-struck crab -apple tree, this sky was more often than not the storm-bringer. Tonight would be yet another example of fine Orcadian weather.

Reluctantly, Hugh Reid turned the prow of his little boat toward Rousay's stony shore. He'd been out too late too many times before, and had since grown accustomed to yielding to the whim of the weather. The early March squalls were often dangerous affairs that too frequently damaged property and threatened the lives of the hardy men and women who made their living on the water. There were signs for their coming, sure, but by the time one recognized them there was usually little time for anything more than a cold-nerved rush to safe harborage.

As Hugh neatly wound his line around his reel, he watched the sky with a wary eye. The old timers who still whispered in fear of the mysteries of Orkney's ghosts and fairies spoke at this time of year of the Mither o' the Sea. Hugh rolled his eyes, reflecting on how reverent grey Sigurd had become at the pub last Thursday. Put a few pints of the Orkney Brewery's latest craft in the man, and when a March hushle picks up he's the first to start in on the story of the Vore Tullye, the fabled battle between the Mither o' the Sea and Teran. The summer goddess' return brings warmth to the seas, calm to the skies, and life to all on the islands, which of course puts her at odds with the winter god of furious gales and mountainous waves. Their struggles for dominance were meant to explain the cruelty of the springtime storms.

Riding high on the swell of one such wave, Hugh Reid scoffed as he always did at the backwardness of such thoughts. Sure, they must have worked in the minds of the ancient Norsemen who had left the marks of their culture all across the islands. But it was the year 2018 and modern meteorology ought to be the explanation now, and for most Orcadians it seemed to be. However, some still preserved the old ways, for reasons Hugh just couldn't fathom. Was it simply an urge to hold to something traditional in the face of the slow creep of modernism on the islands? Or – he mused when the crucifix cut into his line sinker caught his eye – could it be faith?

Well, whatever the reason for the insanity of those rare Orcadians' suppressed beliefs, he could sympathize with the inclination to assign otherworldly origins to this wild weather. The wind turned suddenly, and its voice indeed seemed to howl angrily in his ears as Hugh pulled his oars hard against the water's rough shoves. The sea was too shallow here, the seaweed-shrouded rocks too close to the surface, to make use of his outboard motor. Even rowing was made tricky, and he grimaced when his starboard oar clacked sharply against something unyielding below the surface.

The storm was coming in quickly, which brought some manner of cheer to the fact that his live well remained empty. He'd landed some worthy catches, but nothing that was retainable. Tomorrow he would go to his spot at the lake – Muckle Water – for reliable brown trout, since he'd missed on cod and sea trout today. But first he had to come ashore safely, and when the rain started matting down the wool of his cap Hugh felt a chill of doubt creep spider-like across his flesh.

With a gasping gulp, the water briefly sucked out from under his little craft, giving Hugh a good, heart-stopping glimpse of the rocky ground below him. Just as quickly the sea returned. The fisherman reacted instinctively by pushing his oar handles down hard to lift the blades high out of the surf's reach. Like a gull's plucked wings the oars looked pinioned thus, and like a soaring seabird Hugh's one-man boat rode the back of the gathering wave higher and higher. Grim lines traced his face as he focused on bracing for the flight that was sure to come.

Higher and higher the water carried him; higher and higher until he began to wonder whether the tips of his oars might pierce the bellies of the steel-grey clouds knitting fiercely together overhead. But then something creaked mightily under his seat, and the swell tipped over into a wave. Amidst froth and roar the sea flung Hugh and his craft along the last distance to the shore. The hull of his little boat crashed noisily upon the scree, sliding and slithering several more yards on momentum alone before coming to rest at an angle on its keel. Hugh didn't have long to marvel at the fact that he still had his stomach and bones intact before a growl from behind warned of another building wave.

With a briskness born of necessity, Hugh shipped his oars and leapt from the boat. His wellies scrambled for traction in the shore's loose, gravel-peppered earth as he wrapped a hauling line over his shoulder and leaned into the tension. Only after his boat was out of danger of being swept back to the sea did he pause to catch his breath.

Beginning the walk to where his truck and trailer waited further up the hill, Hugh paused to shake the cold rain out of his eyes. He whisked his hat off, smacking it against the thigh of his waders before plopping it back over his dark hair. The spray of shed water was minimally satisfying, though, as the wool was quickly made sodden once more by the rain. This only surmounted his displeasure of being foolishly caught at sea in a storm at dusk, and he cursed his miscalculation into the crooning wind.

The sound of the skolder softened abruptly, so suddenly that Hugh couldn't help but listen. Underneath the clattering rain was a lilting song so beautiful that he glanced around in vain for some sight of the singer. The grey curtain of the wind-whipped rain denied any such discovery, and after shouting once only to have his voice lost in the noise Hugh gave up the attempt. The song faded back to the forlorn anguish of the storm and he moved on in his quest to retrieve his truck.

Even while he secured his boat on the trailer and

started driving home, the memory of that delicate, beautiful song haunted him. How could such a vicious storm make sounds so resplendent? It made no sense, but what made even less sense was the feeling of nostalgia that he just couldn't shake. Somewhere, somewhen, he felt with certainty that he'd heard that song before. In memories before even his earliest childhood recollections, that alluring lullaby lingered.

"Well," Hugh commented to his rain-fogged windscreen, "it's nothing a dram of whiskey can't fix."

He glanced back once in the mirror to make certain that his boat was still with him after crashing over a rough pothole, but after that his thoughts slid away from the eerie feeling of déjà vu to anticipation of the lamb stew he'd assembled in a crock pot early that morning. The house must smell so nicely, Hugh mused, his otherwise quiet stomach now grumbling hungrily. Thoughts of singing spooks and warring gods were relegated to the back of his mind as he drove through the stormy evening toward a warm meal and comfortable, if lonely, bed.

Gleaming yellow eyes watched his tail-lights disappear into the rain. Their owner crept from an ancient burial mound's entrance, and scowled with a sniffle at the pouring sky. "Ya couldn't let up now? The feller's off the water; no need to keep pissing on down like you are," complained the wizened, wrinkled creature. His words had little effect on the weather, though, except perhaps that it only seemed to worsen. He snorted, and cut a lengthy piece of reed from the trail beside him. The trow muttered a quick phrase under his breath, then lifted his stunted right leg as though to mount the reed; and by the time his foot was raised hip-height the reed had transformed into a white horse whose breath steamed in the cool evening air.

The trow seated himself astride the yellow-eyed beast and kicked it into action. With a distant echo like hooves clattering against cobblestones, the horse leapt into the air, and under the trow's whispered direction and his calloused hands' gentle pressure turned its nose in the direction Hugh's truck had gone.

CHAPTER TWO

The next morning, Hugh woke feeling as though the shadows in the corners of his bedroom were watching him. He lay still for a moment, looking 'round the room. Shrugging off the blankets and the childish fear, he eased out of bed and set about his morning routine of washing up, dressing, and setting a kettle of water on the stove to boil. With each familiar task the uneasiness he'd felt faded until it was nothing more than a lingering suspicion of every movement caught in his peripheral vision. The kettle whistled its readiness and he moved to pour the hot water steadily through the coffee grounds that sat ready in the press. As always, the steam from the water fogged up part of the little kitchen window; and then he saw them: long, narrow hand prints were fresh on the glass.

Hugh leaned closer to investigate, absently tilting the kettle so as not to spill the water on the counter. The palms were child-sized, but had longer fingers than any child's he'd ever seen – and, indeed, longer than any man's or woman's. They were positioned as though to shade one's view when peering inside from without. Hugh set the kettle down and mimicked the gesture; and when he did, he noticed that his mother's necklace was missing. It was an antique silver piece that he'd inherited after her passing. He'd put it on that windowsill after the funeral and had always meant to move it somewhere else but had never quite got around to it. Now it was gone, and the uneasiness from his waking returned full force.

He turned slowly, mechanically, and as he looked around the room he noticed other little details: a chair out of place at the table, a cabinet door slightly ajar, dust and cobwebs cleared out from the corners of the ceiling and floor. Someone had been in his kitchen and swept it, then absconded with his mother's necklace. What else had they taken?

Feeling as though he'd been violated, Hugh prowled cautiously through the rest of the house. In every room something had been moved, but nothing else seemed to be missing. It was simply eerie to think that someone had got into his house while he slept and left it in better order than when they'd come in.

"What manner of thief does such a thing?" Hugh muttered in wonderment.

"One who's not a thief," a gravelly voice croaked in answer. Hugh spun on his heel to scowl into the darkest corner of the living room where an odd little man lounged in Hugh's most comfortable chair. As his eyes adjusted to the lighting, though, Hugh wondered if "creature" wasn't a better term than "man." He was an ugly, stunted thing with pale, wrinkled flesh and gleaming, yellow eyes that reminded Hugh of swamp lights. The calloused hands which clutched his mother's silver necklace, turning the chain methodically among long, narrow fingers, seemed just the right size and shape to make the prints on the kitchen window.

"That's mine," Hugh stated, pointing to the necklace, "and I'll have it back right now."

"Is it?" The creature asked. His yellow eyes looked down at the chain in honest surprise. Then a mischievous mood visibly came over him and the wrinkles at the corners of his eyes deepened. "Maybe it used to be, but I found it and now it's mine. We'll call it payment for cleaning this place up." He whispered a few nonsensical words and twisted his fingers in an impossible gesture, and even as Hugh watched the necklace disappeared. Hugh shook his head briskly to clear his startled wits and to break up the simultaneous pressure between his ears.

Taking advantage of his host's stunned silence, the creature continued: "Now that that's out of the way, is that really how ya greet guests? Because let me tell ya, I'm not terribly pleased about being here in the first place. 'But Kellbrue,' they said, 'you're the one who found the dian-stane anyway. And you're the one who made the trade when he was born. Ya two are linked; now that he's needed, ya must be the one to fetch him.' Well, there's no trow alive who's going to ignore logic like that, so here I am, and there ya are, looking like someone's just walked over your grave. Oi, Hugh Reid, ya can wake up now!"

The situation was so bizarre that Hugh found himself wrapped up in its strangeness, the trespass and theft momentarily forgotten. "You're talking nonsense," he finally protested. "Dian-stanes and trows – that's all stuff out of the old stories, legends made up to frighten children or to explain away things when the reality was too uncomfortable. Did Sigurd put you up to this? Some manner of trick no doubt meant to raise a good laugh at the pub."

"Don't know a Sigurd," his visitor snorted. "But I do know you're very much mistaken, and that's twice now you've insulted me. What nerve, saying that trows are made up nonsense when I'm one sitting here right now talking to ya. Well, not for much longer. There's a Nuggle down at Muckle Water waiting for ya. Tide's rising and the clouds are looking grim. Ya want an explanation? Get down to Muckle Water before the storm breaks, or by then it'll be too late for all of us. Oh, and bring your dian-stane."

"But I don't – "

"It's in your garden path." With that, the trow hopped out of the chair and strode to the door. He opened it to reveal a yellow-eyed, spectral white horse standing ready just outside.

"Don't dally," he advised Hugh before mounting the horse. The beast flickered in the rising sunlight as it leapt into the air, and with a distant sound of hooves on cobblestones it flew away in the direction of a nearby burial mound.

Mystified, Hugh crossed to the door to watch the strange horse and rider descend where the entrance to the howe was hidden by the surrounding turf. Then his gaze drifted skyward and he saw that, sure enough, another storm was gathering over the horizon. How had his mysterious visitor known without looking? Could he really be a trow, a magical creature out of legend, as he claimed? If not, and he was part of some elaborate ruse as Hugh's inner skeptic still suspected, how had he managed the trick of the flying horse? No amount of magician's smoke and mirrors could make that possible, and yet he'd seen with his own eyes the horse launch, fly, and go down to land.

Well, there was one way to verify Kellbrue's claim. Hugh shut the front door and made his way to the back entry, then out into the garden behind the house. Thinking back on the stories he'd heard from Sigurd and the other elders, he recalled that dian-stanes were supposed to be circular and flat, with large holes through their middles. He couldn't remember ever seeing anything like that in his garden, but it wouldn't hurt to look.

A sharp, cold wind burst through the garden, shrieking 'round the low stones that made up its bordering wall. It nipped at Hugh's cheeks and made him shiver in his wool sweater, heavy jeans, and bare feet. As he jammed his hands in his pockets the salty wind tousled the dry weeds' seed-heads, tearing one free to drift and tumble in its wake. Bits scattered loose with each bounce, and Hugh, spellbound, watched it stagger until it stopped, caught by a crack in one of the walkway stones. Compelled by an inexplicable urge, the fisherman ventured from his doorway onto the path. He approached the seed-head and the stone warily, and with each cautious step a tingling suspicion raised the hairs on the back of his neck.

Stooping, he plucked the seed-head up from the ground, and saw that it hadn't come to rest in a crack in the stone at all. Instead its arrest was made by a hole, strangely perfect in its circular shape, in the center of the stone. Hugh dusted the earth slowly from around the edges of the stone, all the while being careful not to touch the paver itself. When he finished uncovering it, he sat back on his heels, kneeling on the path as he stared at what must surely be a dian-stane.

"There's no way this is real," he whispered to himself, and yet the wind seemed to howl laughter in response.

CHAPTER THREE

Hugh knelt there for several minutes, waging an internal battle between life-long disbelief, and the reality that was staring him in the face and almost daring him to blink. Surely any moment now he would wake up in his bed with a blinding hangover and a new, normal day peering around the edges of his window coverings.

The wind died away as quickly as it had come, and as the seconds ticked and Hugh scowled at the stone he realized that its pocked surface was, indeed, familiar. That same eerie nostalgia overcame him as it had when he'd heard the singing on the previous evening. The longer he beheld the stone the more certain he became: he was the one who'd placed it here in the garden path.

Reaching out, Hugh lightly touched the surface of the dian-stane with his fingertips. The cold rock quivered, and in the base of Hugh's brain something primal quivered in response – or, better, in reception. A memory flooded his mind and senses so strongly that Hugh could do nothing but close his eyes and relive it.

He knelt here at this same exact spot and spoke to the stone in his hands. It was bigger then – no, he was smaller, a wee boy. His waking lips moved along with the words he couldn't hear, tingling with the power of them. It was something about "memory" and "when the time of need is at hand once more" and "sleep." On the cracked ground ahead of him his shadow placed the stone into the shallow berth he'd dug for it, and a larger, hunched shadow loomed next to his, watching.

Hugh was released from the memory as suddenly as he'd been taken over by it. A powerful sense of loss reclaimed caused him to tremble on his knees in the path, and with shaking hands he dug the dian-stane from the earth. Where all else the garden was nothing but dry, dead weeds, under the stone's resting place a vibrant circle of soft moss grew; strangely, the soil was barren in the center where the hole in the stone exposed the ground. In his careful grip the stone noticeably warmed. As the seconds ticked on it began to pulse – or the blood flow in his fingers pressed harder against its weight – or both. The combined effect of the warmth and the rhythm gave Hugh the illusion that he was cradling a slumbering young animal rather than a rock, and something within the soul-cage of his chest thrummed with a protective, motherly resonance of familiarity. Whatever else this was, it was his. But how?

"But why?" he asked aloud. Senses reeling as though he were drunk, Hugh lurched suddenly to his feet. This was insane! First, the wild storms and the strange music, then the mysterious visitor straight out of the old-timers' stories, and now this rock and this disturbing return of repressed memories – what did it all mean?

He needed answers, and that meant he needed to follow Kellbrue's suggestion. The trow had said that if he wanted an explanation he should go down to Muckle Water, where a Nuggle waited for him, and that he ought to do it before the coming storm arrived. Did he have time for breakfast? Hugh looked to judge the progression of the storm, and when he did his heart sank. Just like it had last evening the system was moving far too quickly for something natural. Sure, Orcadian storms were renowned for their ferocity and their ability to brew up seemingly out of nowhere, but those heavy, black clouds were halfway across the island at this point. That was fast even by Orcadian storm standards.

As Hugh watched, the horizon smeared, smudged by the grey curtain of rain which began to fall from the clouds. The wind returned, twisting in from the direction of the storm, and it carried the promise of heavy rain in its scent.

"No time for breakfast, then," Hugh muttered darkly, the words almost a curse themselves. For a man who made his living by working all day from his fishing boat, breakfast was an important part of fortifying himself for the day. To miss this crucial event was essentially sacrilegious to the fisherman. However, if he wanted to beat this storm to Muckle Water, he could not afford to spend the time such a thorough meal required.

Cradling the dian-stane in the crook of his left arm, Hugh rushed into the house. He pulled a protein bar from one of the boxes in his pantry, not willing to skip the meal altogether. He kept these bars for use as a quick hunger fix on the boat, but today one would serve to solve the problem of his shortened meal time. Leaving the kettle to cool on the stone counter, he slammed the front door shut behind him, unhitched his boat trailer, and piled into the driver's seat of his truck. Hugh pulled out of the gravel driveway with a tire-spinning urgency. Pointing his truck south-east he dropped the dian-stane onto his passenger seat and sped toward Muckle Water. As he one-handedly worked the food bar free of its packaging, Hugh glanced at his rear view mirror to gauge the storm's progress – and what he saw shocked him.

The thunderhead had doubled in size from mere minutes ago. Without any noticeable increase in the winds the shadow of its rain curtain had inexplicably jumped closer to Hugh's location. A tight anxiety gripped his stomach, and even if Kellbrue hadn't advised him thus Hugh knew with an instinctive certainty that he must win the race to Muckle Water. He pressed hard on the gas pedal so that his truck roared and bounced even faster over the pock-mark pot holes that littered the island road.

Lightning flared out across the black storm clouds, painting a temporarily brilliant lace pattern in its wake. The terrified urgency it left in Hugh was only heightened by the purring roll of thunder that followed it.

"I can't believe I'm even doing this," Hugh grumbled around a bite. The granola in the bar was bitterly stale, or maybe his nerves made it taste so, but he swallowed the morsel nonetheless and pursued another. It, too, was like dust in his mouth.

"I – this is ridiculous," he complained to his silent passenger for lack of a better audience. At least the dian-stane wouldn't talk back. "There probably won't be anything at the lake. I'll just be one more simple fool caught out in the weather." But Hugh was plagued by a tenacious curiosity that wouldn't allow him to go back home to hide his head under his pillow. He had to see this through, even if there wasn't anything in this adventure except madness. That's all he expected: nothing at the lake but a soaking rain to wash his truck and a compelling reason to either stop drinking completely or triple the dose.

That is, unless a mythical Nuggle really did wait for him there, and the old men with their nonsensical stories were right all along. A boyish giddiness curled his toes at the idea. It was the unknown – the "what if" – that made him push his speedometer needle well past the legal limit.

Not soon enough, the curving edge of the lakeshore came glimmering into view. Lightning skittered across the charging clouds again and again, pulsing like a heartbeat – like his own quickened heartbeat, Hugh realized. It skipped a beat as his panic reached new heights. Thunder broke so loudly it made the steering wheel vibrate in Hugh's hands as the truck shook in the wake of the clap. And then, as he brought the truck to a gravel-slinging, brakes-grinding stop, he saw it: the impossible Nuggle. Its pale fur glistened wetly, with dark trails tracing down its neck, sides, and withers where the water ran, streaming and inexplicably source-less, from the green kelp-strands of its mane. Its seaweed tail wafted in the wind-stoked wavelets that lapped around its knees. It watched him with stern blue eyes over soft nostrils that leaked a foggy mist with each huffing breath. The water-horse snorted once, and tossed its mighty head impatiently.

<THERE IS NO TIME FOR AWE, HUGH REID,> proclaimed a soundless voice inside the fisherman's head. Nonetheless Hugh heard it, clearer between his ears than

anything he'd heard in his life.

"What is … " he started to ask, and the Nuggle snorted again, confirming Hugh's suspicion that the voice was the legendary horse's, sent psychically.

<THERE IS NO TIME. IF YOU WANT YOUR QUESTIONS ANSWERED, WARDEN OF THE STONE, GET ON MY BACK. WE MUST LEAVE NOW. NOW!>

CHAPTER FOUR

That sort of abrupt, arrogant answer made Hugh's lip curl with irritation, but he withheld the churlish response that came immediately to mind. The Nuggle was right in its claim. Rolling in on winds that frothed the narrow lake, the unnatural storm was almost upon them. Hugh could taste the metallic smell of incoming rain with each panting breath.

Never sparing a second to roll his window up – the crank didn't work anyway – Hugh killed the truck's engine and left the keys swinging in the ignition. He always hoped that someone might steal it and he could use the insurance payout to get a new one, but no one seemed interested in the clunker. Grabbing the dian-stane up from the threadbare passenger seat, Hugh opened the cab door. A ferocious guster nearly tore the door from his grasp, and he quickly slammed it shut behind his exit.

The water-horse pawed at the waves as Hugh waded through the shallows to its side. There, though, he balked at the height of the kelp-draped monster's withers.

"Look, I've never ridden a horse, much less a ..." Hugh protested, and waved vaguely at the Nuggle when his words trailed off.

Luckily, the Nuggle seemed to care more about making a hasty exit than insisting on maintaining a regal stance. It knelt in the shallows, one heavy leg at a time bent so as to lower its back to an easier height. Hugh recalled the stories of this creature as he looked upon the damp hide: it was said that finmen, the dark oarmasters of the depths, were the only beings who could ride a Nuggle safely. All others were carried out to deep water and drowned.

As if it guessed at his thoughts and the reason for his hesitation, the Nuggle snorted impatiently again. <IF KELLBRUE MEANT YOU TO DROWN, THE TROW WOULD HAVE DONE THE DEED HIMSELF. YOU ARE NEEDED ON HETHER BLETHER, HUGH REID. TERAN MUST BE OVERCOME AND THE VORE TULLYE FINISHED. THE MITHER O' THE SEA REQUIRES YOUR ASSISTANCE TO DIMINISH HIM. BUT THERE WILL BE TIME FOR ANSWERS SOON – FOR NOW YOU MUST RIDE!>

Lightning hissed down to the water ten meters to Hugh's left, exploding in a rush of light and steam and thunder. Reacting blindly, Hugh grasped the Nuggle's slick mane and slung his leg over its back to sit just behind its withers. The water-horse lunged to its feet immediately in a rush of sea-sawing movement. Hugh clung to its back, one arm clutching the dian-stane to his stomach as the steam rose around them and thickened into a mist. When he noticed a peculiar salty smell, quite out of place in this fresh-water loch, Hugh realized the Nuggle must be behind the cold sea-mist.

The water-horse surged into motion, and Hugh found himself oddly comfortable as it wheeled and ploughed into deeper water. In some manner of thoughtfulness – Hugh doubted it was necessity – it kept its head and back above the chill surface of the water. Even then, the spray from its wake reached Hugh's face, and he could taste the increasing saltiness of their bath. Somehow they were moving from the land-locked loch to the sea, and he wagered that the Nuggle's mist was responsible for transporting them.

Slowly, the mist thinned, and as Hugh squinted around him he glimpsed a shoreline approaching. The prevalent sound of waves breaking on sand made him aware that his hearing had been muffled in the mist. A channel marker bemoaned its presence off to their left, startling Hugh. He twisted to find it, and proclaimed, "We're just off Rousay! That's not Mainland…is that Eynhallow?" He asked the Nuggle.

Its reply in his head held a note of tired amusement. <NO, HUGH REID. WHEN ONCE THE MIST WAS NEEDED TO COME TO EYNHALLOW, THE IRON RELIGION OF MAN HAS ANCHORED IT FAST TO THE MORTAL REALM. NO, WHAT LIES BEFORE YOU IS HETHER BLETHER, WHICH RESIDES IN EYNHALLOW'S SHADOW. HERE YOU WILL STILL FIND MAGIC AND MIRACLES.>

They drew closer to the shore and there the mist fully broke. White buildings gleamed in the sunlight; white sands glittered with a gem-like beckoning. The clean, stark beauty of the simple thatched homes and sheds seemed too extreme to be normal. Hugh's heart ached with a desire and a longing such as he'd never felt before, and it rose swelling within him as they rode the filling tide. It was a blended emotion that he couldn't quite place. He felt as though he was looking at something that had been stolen from him, and now the thief was trying to sell it back.

A barking sound startled him from his confusion, and Hugh turned his gaze to the seal whose round head broke the waves beside them. The whiskered beast studied him with wide, black eyes before darting on ahead. Hugh watched it pass effortlessly through the water – and he noticed now that tens – no, hundreds of the mottled animals had appeared. Their heads dotted the sea, and here and there flippers splashed in their game, and here and there a sparkle of fish scales caught the fisherman's attention.

The flukes were alluring: silver edged with shifting shades of green, purple, blue and yellow. They transitioned to a gracefully curved, powerful tail, which swept up to a pale-fleshed waist and belly. Hugh identified the creature instantly when her perfect breasts and streaming, blonde hair came into view: mermaid. Every waterman knew the stories and dangers of the mermaid. As she turned, rolling in the water with a luscious swirl of her arms, her eyes met his. Her face lifted out of the sea, seal-dark eyes gleaming wetly, and her lips parted invitingly. The Nuggle felt Hugh's weight move on its back as he leaned down toward the temptress. Before the Nuggle could warn Hugh, however, the mermaid's large, black eyes narrowed suspiciously. She shrieked a horrible keen before thrashing down and away. All of the flickers of fish scales flitted away, and some of the seals vanished too. The ones that stuck with them began to bark short, rasping chuffs that seemed too close to laughter to be anything else. Hugh gripped the Nuggle's slimy kelp mane with his free hand, twisting at the waist to scan the sea for the mermaid.

"Where'd she go?" he questioned frantically.

<YOU'RE OF NO INTEREST TO A MERMAID, HUGH REID,> the Nuggle replied. <TO KEEP HER YOUTH AND HER BEAUTY SHE NEEDS TO MATE A MORTAL MAN, AND TOO BECOME MORTAL.>

"But I am a mortal man," Hugh countered, rocking on the Nuggle's back as its hooves hit ground. It rose, splashing through the rest of the wave breaks until it stood upon the shore of the last vanishing isle. Hugh slid gracelessly off the Nuggle's back and would have pushed his argument but for the sight of a tall, swarthy fellow stomping across the sand toward them.

"What are you thinking, bringing him here?" The man shouted coarsely. His sinewy features were wrinkled in a most unpleasant way.

<I BROUGHT HIM NOWHERE HIS HEART DOESN'T ALREADY KNOW,> the Nuggle replied, stepping forward a pace so that his shoulder was in front of Hugh. <THE TROW SUMMONED HIM TO ASSIST WITH THE VORE TULLYE. HE IS A WARDEN.>

The cloaked man scowled at Hugh – or, more directly, at the dian-stane that he held tightly to his chest. "What trow?" He spat, lips curling over yellow, broken teeth.

"Kellbrue," Hugh answered, and the dark man's glare swept up to the fisherman's eyes.

"Kellbrue!" He snarled. "That sentimental fool. The Vore Tullye will proceed as it has every year without a Warden's help. It is the natural progression of things! Kellbrue will answer for his meddling." The cloaked man snapped his long, bony fingers and a howling wind spun up around them. Hugh's stomach clenched with the nauseating effect of sudden, unbelievably fast movement, and even as he put pressure to his guts and mouth in reaction the gale vanished.

He blinked vision back to his tearing eyes and staggered after the cloaked man. The Nuggle was no longer in their company, a fact which Hugh almost didn't take notice of. Solid dirt was under his feet again rather than shifting sands, and it made a natural sort of sense that a water creature like the Nuggle would have been excluded from the travel method that had brought them here.

The gale deposited them at the entrance to a barrow. A tunnel into the hill opened before them and the disgruntled man stormed down that tunnel. His long legs set a pace that lanky Hugh appreciated. Just as the light left them in pitch black the tunnel turned abruptly and yawned into a huge, well-lit cavern decorated with silver trinkets. Spirited jig music somehow filled the impossible acoustics of the space.

Hugh blinked hard again to adjust his eyes to the change of light. Gazing in wonder at the myriad shining treasures, he followed the cloaked man further into the room.

"Kellbrue!" His guide shouted, but his summons was drowned immediately by the fairy reels. "KELLBRUE!" He tried again, dark face becoming ruddy with the effort, and a few spritely dancers turned to look in their direction. Creatures of all manner of make-believe romped and gamboled to the inspired fiddle music. That is, until the cloaked man snarled and lifted his twisted fingers into the air.

The source-less lights dimmed, and Hugh's ears popped under a sudden pressure change. The musicians' fiddles and bodhrans twisted, popping strings and skins as the wood shrank under the touch of salt.

"KELLBRUE!" The cloaked man barked a third time, and his voice now filled the startled silence. "Come, trow! Give reason for your meddling, or so help me I will..."

"Careful, sorcerer. Var, the Oath-keeper, is among you in my house this day." The response was Kellbrue's voice.

The cloaked man gathered spittle in his throat, but decided against evacuating that rude noise on the shale floor. "You have brought a Warden to Hether Blether without my consent," he accused, and slowly the crowd of revelers parted to give a clear sightline to the trow leaning against a hearthside slate shelf. "Moreover, you have brought THIS Warden!" He roared, and pointed a crooked finger at Hugh. "What game are you playing, trow? I find it not at all amusing!"

"First of all," Kellbrue replied, his voice strategically bored, "I have brought no one to Hether Blether. That was the Nuggle, if you like. Secondly, this year's Vore Tullye is not transpiring as normal. We've all seen the storms, sorcerer. Even a finman of your caliber dares not put a boat on the water of late. The Sea Mither needs a Warden, and yours is the only one left. Trust me, I looked."

Hugh had finally had enough of the way they all seemed to be hinting at him with vague connections and titles. "Yours?" He interrupted, clutching at the dian-stane while taking a step away from the cloaked man. "I have been dragged from my home and rushed away under threats, and I am not some trout to be held by the lip and measured. Stop talking about me like I'm not here and like I'm something I'm not. I'm not his Warden, his anything! I didn't even believe in…until you…I swear, if I don't get some bloody answers right now I'll walk out and swim home and you can solve your problem yourselves!" His tirade raised the Scottish fire in his blood and reddened his cheeks.

A woman – or close enough – near Kellbrue stirred when Hugh said 'I swear.' From behind her head and beneath her skin a golden light softly began to glow as he blustered. At the end of Hugh's tirade, she smiled sadly. "You will do no such thing, Warden," she rebutted.

Huffing, Hugh stomped his foot. The alternative was to give way to frustrated tears and he would not allow that to happen.

"I will!" He shouted, ears warming as he realized how childish that sounded.

"The Oath-keeper reads Truths, Hugh Reid, and she is

never wrong. But go ahead. Give your dian-stane to me and leave if you can." Kellbrue called his bluff. The answer he got was unexpected.

When his possession of the stone was compromised, Hugh's brows knitted into a frown. His scowl almost hid the way the darkness of his pupils seemed to swell, overcoming the whites of his eyes.

"No!" He growled firmly. The earth of the howe around them rumbled in echo, and dust ran out in a line between him and the cloaked man and the rest of the assembly. It followed a new crack in the slate floor.

"Protect your own, then, like a good Warden," the trow sneered.

Hugh's eyes cleared, and he stared aghast from the stone to the crack to the sorcerer, who glared solemnly at him. When the fisherman's gaze came finally to Kellbrue, it was braced with determination and only a little, well-shielded fear. This was all confusing and unknown, but he was a man of Orkney. Better yet, he was a Rousay Reid. He steeled himself, and bade the trow, "Explain."

CHAPTER FIVE

"It's not so much my story to tell as it belongs to the Finman beside you."

"You had as much a hand in this as anyone, Kellbrue."

"Well, regardless, I'm a better storyteller than you are anyway, sorcerer. You, Hugh Reid, are a changeling child."

"A security measure."

"Call it what you will, what you did was still stealing, sorcerer. See, Hugh Reid, when you were born your father here took you from your crib on Hether Blether and brought you to iron Rousay. There, a wee human bairn had also just recently been born; right down to the same minute as you, in fact. I - well, no matter. I got what was due to me, and swapped you with the human whelp. He left you there, barely a few hours old: too young and too familiar for the new parents to know any different. He brought the human baby here and raised him to be the perfect mate for his selkie daughter."

"You have no right to judge me, trow."

"I'm just telling a story, old crook. Anyway, when you were born, Hugh Reid, the earth shook and the winds wailed and stars fell and cattle died and I've since learned there were seven stillborn lambs produced that night. Seven! That's strong in the omen world. So when I say I acted on a hunch, that's what I thought at the time. I've been a minion of fate more than once.

"What I mean to say, Hugh Reid, is that you were always meant to find that dian-stane. It is the last of the stones created on the Faroe Islands, and it is linked to your very essence. You've probably always felt drawn to it, whether you knew it or not. Maybe you hid it from his eyes, sorcerer, but even you should know that is not the way of talismans. Eventually, they sing to those who are matched to them. That stone protects you from attacks - did you not wonder why Teran's storm never quite wreaked its havoc upon you? It was delayed by your stone, by your will and desire to keep it at bay. Legend says it may serve to focus great power. And we are the stuff of legends, so we ought to know.

"It's also no coincidence that you took to being a fisherman. If nothing else finmen are unrivaled at the oar so you were destined to do something on the water. But I'm just a meddling trow. I'll let your father here teach you about finman things."

"He'll work it out himself or not at all, Kellbrue."

"That's hardly fair, sorcerer, but so be it. Now, the reason I sought you out again after all these irrelevant years: the Vore Tullye. You see, Hugh Reid, there is an immortal struggle happening behind the scenes of the seasons. Once a year the Mither o' the Sea returns to warm the waters and ease the lives of her favorite children who poison the waters and leech the land. She fights so fiercely with Teran, old man winter, and every year she binds him to the sea floor and heals the traumas wreaked by their conflict. We see bounteous spring and bright summer, and all the while Teran screams and shakes and savages his bindings. His too-temporary shackles break, and he lunges free to battle once more. Thus we see the autumn storms, the Gore Vellye, until the Mither is bested and shunned and winter reigns again. We watch, we wait, and the cycle turns.

"But not so this year. You may have noticed the spring storms are taking a higher toll this year. They should have eased by now, for the Mither has chained Teran twice already. Each time he responded with such a fury that he shattered the earth. The Mither's strength is waning as she struggles with Teran, and if she does not conquer him this third time we fear there will not be a fourth battle. Winter will have conquered summer, and the world will descend into a darkness the likes of which we shall not survive. There are things in the dark and the cold, Hugh Reid. They look out from the horizon at the hour of civil dusk, when the sun is just below the edge of the water but not yet extinguished. They tread the shadows of night, the Old Ones, and they push at the veil when it is at its thinnest. One or two have walked among mortal men before - giants, Jotun, now encased in stone upon the isles - but the last was stopped hundreds of years ago. Or so we thought.

"Teran cannot be this strong on his own. The Mither needs help to make him submit, and we need you to help her. You are a Finman, master of the sea, and you are a Warden of the Stones. You are probably the least of both of these, but such a combination has never been seen before. You must learn, Hugh Reid, and you must do it quickly. Orkney was once a place where ordinary men became legends. It is time for this to happen again.

"Back on your island, your Rousay, there is a spae-wife called Hulda. Seek her out, and mind you don't keep her waiting because she probably already knows you're coming. She is kin to the reindeer folk, the Saami, and she is one of the few technically mortal witches who has seen a giant turned to stone by the warmth of the sun. Yetnasteen, your Rousay people named him, which by the way is unfairly obtuse, referring to a petrified giant as "Giant Stone." Seek her out, for if anyone were equipped to teach you the dian-stane's use, it is Hulda. Seek her out-"

"A falsehood, Kellbrue. You aim, as always, to dig a thorn in my side. You antagonise me with his presence."

"If that is so, sorcerer, it is a happy coincidence. My sole purpose in inviting Hugh Reid here was to explain to him exactly as I have done; provided by your bluster or not it would have occurred. So, Hugh Reid, seek out the spae-wife Hulda, or doom the world to a relentless rime. It is not so much an ultimatum as it is a guarantee of what will happen should you fail."

CHAPTER SIX

Hugh was overcome by a sudden dizziness, and he sank into a chair that one of the observing revelers moved within his range. Yesterday these things, these trows and finfolk and giants and the Mither o' the Sea, and all of it; yesterday these things were just the dusty stories dusty men spoke of over the tart mouths of their cups. But how could he deny what Kellbrue claimed when he'd outrun an ungodly storm on the back of a Nuggle? How could he cry nonsense when he'd traveled by lightning to the brownie's barrow? How could these things be merely stories? Oh, the lads would laugh when he returned to the pub and told them so. Or would they? They kept dwelling on the stories not for joy of the telling but for fear of the truths that lay behind them. Would the wizened fools welcome him to their company or, knowing his fae-touched truth, would they face him with an iron crucifix and a harsh banishing word? Hugh suddenly wasn't as keen to find out.

"I'm sure it's a blow to the bonnet," Kellbrue was saying, "but I'm afraid there's no time to sit around and ponder oblivion. Oblivion's knocking at the door, as it were, and we need you to lift the bar into place."

"How do I get back?" Hugh inquired. His waking posture indicated that he'd finally mentally signed on to the monumental task asked of him.

"To Rousay or here?" Kellbrue questioned.

"Well, Rousay, but I suppose… " Hugh began, but Kellbrue interrupted him.

The trow riddled, "To one you must find your way

yourself, while the other shall propose itself."

The cloaked man rolled his eyes as Hugh scowled at the puzzle. "I think you've spun enough mystery, Kellbrue. Warden, you shall return to Rousay on my ferry. I am sure when all is said and done you will have discovered how to go to your home. Whether or not it will be there for your arrival, well, we shall see."

They turned their backs to Kellbrue when the trow stuck his tongue out and gestured for the musicians to strike up their reel once more. Upon exiting the howe, the cloaked man put his crook-fingered hand to the nape of Hugh's neck; instinctively Hugh lifted his foot to step forward - and he placed it down not on grassy turf but on the diamond-bright beach to which the Nuggle had delivered him. He staggered slightly on the softer terrain, his footing challenged by the sorcerer's unwavering march that forced him to continue down the beach to the shoreline. There was no sign of the waterhorse, but another thought took primary concern in Hugh's mind.

"Can I meet him?" He requested of the cloaked man.

"Who?" Grunted his pilot as their feet touched salt water. Hugh halted, instinctively waiting while the sorcerer waded out to a boat anchored in the shallows. Like a whale's sweeping flukes the sorcerer's robes spread in the waters around his thighs. His hands hefted the anchor line as though it were feather-light; the stone at the end thumped on the deck. Shafts of light cut askance on a rush of wavelets; in the same mood, Hugh studied the ferry-boat suspiciously. Its creaking, salt-bleached boards seemed hardly suitable for use in a duck pond.

"The other changeling," he clarified. "The one you brought here for your daughter to marry."

The cloaked man climbed into the boat, water rushing from his garments as he mounted the side. He settled abruptly to the oarsman's bench, and his reply was just as final. "No."

"No?" Hugh echoed, startled by the denial when he'd only just begun to receive answers. Scores of terns cried out along the shore, and in their noise he heard it repeated: no, no, no. "Why not?"

The sorcerer lifted his weather-creased face and beckoned for Hugh to board the ferry. He held the boat steady with a gentle play of the oars, balancing the pitch of Hugh's graceless weight with his seat at the locks. Everything about his presence in the boat was masterful and confident, fueled with a power that Hugh could just barely sense.

With his passenger seated at the bow the ferryman parted his cracked lips to explain: "Because he is dead."

Taking advantage of Hugh's shocked silence, the cloaked man leaned into his oars and pulled the boat out to sea. He rowed mutely into the thickening ocean fog. Soon all around them was obscured, so that even the sun's glow overhead dimmed to that queer half-light displayed during the time of civil dusk. The sound of the world faded behind the weighty cotton-cloud until all that was left was the slap of salt crests against the hull and the patient rasp of the oars. It was quietude so somber that it seemed irresponsible to break it, and so Hugh withheld his questions. Judging by the focused creases on the cloaked man's face, he probably wouldn't gain any answers if he did dare to ask them. The ocean rolled endlessly beneath the boat, and the oars groaned high and low, high and low, to the rhythm of the ticking second hand that had stopped in Hugh's wristwatch years ago. Hugh huddled his shoulders against the eerie calm. The metronomic repetition might be enough to drive a man mad if it wasn't so blithely hypnotizing.

A gull coasted through their humdrum bubble. It cried out a solitary, plaintive note and wheeled overhead before it soared away, vanishing into the mists in the same direction of the ferry's heading. Its wingtips cut trails in the otherworldly fog, disturbing the cloaked man's shroud. Swirls and eddies flushed down the trails and the barrier thinned to a haze, then nothing. Landfall appeared before them. Waves leapt and frothed over haggard beaches in action so rough that Hugh at first did not recognize their landing. But then it came to him: they were on the eastern side of Rousay, just north of the ferry lines. This was the Rousay Sound in fine, stormy temper, and there the Burn of Cruar sliced into the land. They had just accomplished a multi-hour journey in minutes. Hugh, shocked, looked 'round to the cloaked man, whose smug face seemed expectant of that reaction. He gave one more hearty pull of the oars before heaving the anchor stone over the side.

"You'll swim from here," the ferryman announced.

Dismayed, Hugh visually measured the distance to the shore. Under calm conditions, it would have been no trouble. But with the current state of the rioting sea, he wasn't looking forward to the exertion.

"Why? There's plenty of depth to get in closer." He rebutted.

"This is as close to the Iron Land that I will go," the cloaked man replied. There was something in his voice that brought Hugh's curious gaze back to him.

"Will, or can?" the fisherman questioned. He was met with an unyielding, dark stare. Hugh sighed. "I suppose it doesn't matter, then. I don't have a bag for the stone," he added weakly.

"Lie adrift upon your back and the sea will take you to shore," came the impassive response.

Understanding that this was the way it would be, Hugh vented his discontent with another, louder sigh. But he collected the dian-stane in a strong double-armed embrace against his chest and, taking a deep breath, committed himself to the current.

CHAPTER SEVEN

Waves swept over his head, then broke; he clamped his lips tight against the swell, then breathed. He opened his eyes once and straightaway closed them again. The sky rolled; his stomach rolled; he screwed his eyes tightly shut. Hugh attempted to measure the time by counting rises and falls, but it was no good. How many should he expect?

The scything current seemed to divert more harshly when he worried that he might be drifting off course. He focused his mind on his destination, on the shore, and someone named Hulda, and - wonder of wonders - his carriage calmed and the sea smoothed. In moments the ocean gave a final surge to berth him upon the shale.

That is where she found him. Still with his eyes closed he lay belly-up, laughing aloud, absolutely out of his mind with glee, amazement, and the utter helplessness of a man who has surrendered himself to the realization that the world is so much bigger than he wanted to believe. It was the sort of laughter that is the only option when crying is all that is left.

"Hugh Reid?" She asked, unable to suppress a sympathetic chuckle of her own.

The castaway opened his eyes and beheld her with a fatigued, bloodshot gaze. The woman looked to be of his own age range, though her eyes were framed by the wrinkles of a wisdom beyond that. She wore a white tunic over a white skirt, the hems of which drifted in the sea foam splashing around his prone body. A blue coat hung

43

open on her shoulders, and a gold braid belted her billowy shirt to give it form at the waist. A necklace of clear gems garnished her throat, and the rays of the sun were captured there and set them a-glow as with an internal fire. Falcon plumes littered her wheat-yellow hair, no doubt tied in but seemingly natural as the wind tousled strand and feather alike.

"Aye," Hugh confirmed. "I suppose you'll be Hulda?"

"For you," she answered with a cat-like smile, "that name will serve just fine."

CHAPTER EIGHT

Hugh felt every crashing wave in his head as the ocean pounded its fury against the rocky shore. He was cold, and his pants slapped wetly against his legs as he followed the shining white figure ahead of him. He was so cold that he couldn't feel the exertion pain that burned through his body.

They walked through an empty pasture and crossed the first wire fence. Some white-fleeced sheep occupied the second pasture, and they lifted their faces sleepily as Hulda and Hugh slogged by. Crossing a second wire fence, they came into a third pasture. Lambs peeked curiously around their mothers' sides, watching intently while the pair passed. Seed-heads of tall grasses were turned away at Hulda's hem, and Hugh followed doggedly down the path her bare feet traced in the sod. They stepped over the third fence and touched pavement. Looking left and right by habit, Hugh recognized the B9064, a road that he had little to do with on a daily basis but which he'd travelled frequently enough.

Across the road, a footpath climbed up the rising hill. Hulda headed to it, which puzzled Hugh's ocean-addled sense. He paused, and noticing his dalliance she looked back with a questioning expression.

"Well, there's just a ruin," he stated, gesturing at the crumbling stone husk that lurked behind the unkempt hedge just past the disheveled stone wall. Weeds and brambles ran amuck, and brown moss carpeted the places where pieces of the shingled roof had fallen in.

Hulda made a clicking sound with her tongue against her pallet, shaking her head as she came back to him. "I can tell you have much to learn indeed, Hugh Reid. Close your eyes," she commanded. Hugh obeyed. He felt her fingertips lightly touch his eyelids, and the dian-stane warmed in his grasp.

"Now look again," bade Hulda.

What Hugh saw when he reopened his eyes was starkly different from the ruin. Instead, a quaint stone house stood in its place, fully intact with a warm, flickering glow radiating from every window. The hedge was still wild but the garden wall was complete and orderly. Hulda guided Hugh into the garden, which thrived with all manner of herb and vegetable, some of which Hugh had never seen before. Gazing upon the lush bounty of green, growing things, Hugh remembered his barren yard with its cracked pavers and was overcome with a vicious sense of guilt. It was almost enough to distract him from the odd effect happening in his peripheral vision. The illusion returned in his indirect sight, so that if he stared straight at the beautifully leaded windows of the cottage, then in the corner of his eye the garden wall was again a neglected wreck.

Whether she perceived his confusion or she was planning to provide an explanation anyway, Hulda clarified, "That illusion is called a 'seeming'; it makes something seem like something else. I will teach you to see Truly, for you will need this skill in the fight against Teran."

They crossed the road and continued up the footpath into the front garden. A low growl drew Hugh's eye to the wall's shade where a huge, grey tomcat lounged. The tip of the bear-like feline's tail switched to and fro, and he stared suspiciously at Hugh the way only cats can. The bright green eyes remained fixated on him even when Hulda uttered, "Hush now, he's welcome here. This is Hugh Reid, the Finman's Warden. Come in," she beckoned to Hugh, who followed her over the cottage's threshold. Another massive cat occupied the surface of the wooden kitchen table, which was the first thing Hugh noticed. The table looked immeasurably heavy and was riddled with knots and tradesman's marks from when it was hand-hewn. On its worn surface sprawled the second biggest cat Hugh had ever seen, though to be fair it was only a smidge smaller than the grey tom out in the garden. His eyes matched the grey's with an eerie exactness, and if it weren't for the precisely pointed ears that turned to acknowledge every sound then this tomcat's tabby stripes would have convinced Hugh that its heritage was part tiger.

"Off! Go on, off!" Hulda hissed to the tabby. The feline leisurely rose, stretching every muscle in his sizeable frame as he watched her cross to the stovetop. Licking his whiskers after a yawn, he piled his hindquarters in a sit, tail curling around to drape over his paws. Filling a bowl with the contents of the simmering pot, Hulda brought it and a spoon to the table. She gave the tabby a firm shove in his ribs, which earned her a disapproving "mrow." However, the cat abandoned the table with a jump to the top of the nearby icebox.

Hugh had lingered in the entrance to watch these events. The physical and emotional exertions of the day were catching up to him, so that when he eased into the chair that Hulda pulled out for him he wondered whether he'd be able to get up from it. The seat was a simple wooden affair, unadorned but functional, but after the day he'd just had it was the most comfortable thing Hugh had ever sat on.

The stew was a brothy mixture of garden greens and beans that Hugh guessed had been plucked fresh from the plants just past the cottage's stone walls. He ate it mechanically with one hand holding the dian-stane on his lap. After a few silent minutes, Hulda offered, "You can put the stone under your chair. This is the place where it was enchanted," she chided his possessive scowl. "It shan't move except by your doing."

Chagrined, Hugh recalled everything Kellbrue had said about Hulda. He leaned down and tucked the dian-stane under his chair. By the time he finished his bowl of stew exhaustion had fully taken hold of his mind and body. Hulda perceived the way his head and shoulders dipped lower and the way his blinks took longer. "There is little time to spare," she cautioned, smilingly, "but if we do not take time to rest then we shall not make it to the end. A room is ready for you abovestairs, Hugh Reid. Go up and sleep, and we will begin your training early on the morrow."

Her advice was sound and Hugh willingly followed it.

He carried his bowl to the sink and rounded the corner
where the narrow staircase was lit by the smoky glow of
two oil lamps. The red and green fuel shone gem-like
under the burning wicks. Hugh stood with his hand on the
rail for a minute, watching the way the emerald shadows
marbled the white-washed walls, before he realized that
some of that color was actually filtering in from outside.
He bypassed the stairs, going out the back door, and gazed
in awe at the green-blue aurora that filled the night sky.
Molten mint and columbine cavorted over the hill to the
northwest and the sea to the northeast. The lights seemed
to undulate in a rhythm that matched the chirruping of the
crickets. Hugh had seen the aurora plenty of times before,
but this occurrence was different. A heavy peace eased
him down onto the stoop, where he sat calmly with his
forearms propped on his knees and his hands dangling
above his flat-planted feet. Time seemed to calm from its
rushing pace, and the world settled into stillness with him.
And all the while the beryl sky burned.

CHAPTER NINE

"Today," Hulda announced over the crackling of lamb sausage frying in the pan, "you will meet a giant."

"There's no such thing," Hugh remarked over his glass of goat milk. He kept a wary eye on the grey tomcat that lounged on the table at the other side of his formerly egg-filled plate. The cat had woken him up this morning by standing all of weight on Hugh's trachea. Hulda had assured him that the feline hadn't done so with murderous intent, but Hugh wasn't convinced.

Realizing that Hulda was staring hard at him, Hugh looked up at her. "Well, there isn't!" He shrilled, even though he knew by her expression that he must be incorrect. "I think I'd have noticed a bloody giant stomping around Rousay."

Hulda sniffed her disapproval as she plucked the sausages off the heat. "Now is not the time to resort to belligerence, Hugh Reid. You slept through an earthquake in the early hours. Teran is close to breaking free again, and though it was a minor quake it is a sign of the Mither's slipping control. We must attend directly to your training, and you must accept my word as true. Ask how, where, when, even why, but by now you should be aware of the fact that there are hidden things in your world. I never said there were giants 'stomping around Rousay;' I said that today you will meet one."

"It was just a reflex," Hugh grumbled, bristling in his embarrassment. He chewed on a sausage and a thought. Hadn't Kellbrue talked of a giant that Hulda had witnessed being turned to stone? "It's not what's-his-name, is it? Yetnasteen?"

"Of course, Kellbrue must have told you. The trow does enjoy sharing others' stories so. Though that is not his true name, Yetnasteen shall serve. Yes, that is the giant that you will meet."

"How, if he's frozen in stone?"

"I shall unfreeze him."

Hugh gulped, nearly choking on his sausage. "Is that a good idea?"

Hulda smirked. "For you, probably not. But I locked him into that stone that bears his name, and so I am the keeper of his key. Handling Teran's giants will be your task in the battle to come. You will not want those to be your first giants. Fueled by frost and fury, they are much tougher game than the hermits of the hills."

"Kellbrue said the sun turned Yetnasteen to stone, and that you only observed it."

"Did he? Well, Kellbrue is either mixing his giants with his trolls, or he gave you a half-truth like he so loves to do. The sun turned Yetnasteen to stone because, with the Mither's blessing, I cleared the clouds to let it through. Have you ever worked the weather, Hugh Reid?"

She shook her head. "No, but you will one day. It is something we avoid interfering with, because to encourage much-needed rain in one place may upset the balance and cause drought in another place. To tweak the wind and clear clouds may produce a tornado if not done properly. But with precious care it can be done beautifully. Finish your breakfast and meet me in the back garden when you've done."

White skirt swirling at her bare heels, she left him to his meal. The grey tomcat followed her out, paws padding lightly in the trail of the glimmers that reflected off her gold-braid belt. Hugh ate under the silent, watchful eye of the tabby cat lounging on top of the icebox. As felines do, Hulda's sizeable companions always seemed to be nonchalantly at ease. However, something in their beryl eyes assured Hugh that they could go from supine to savage with minimal provocation. The way they watched him promised that they were just waiting for an excuse to switch from mild to murderous.

Almost as though he could hear Hugh's ruminations, the tabby stretched his paws. Toes reached individually wide, bear-like claws sliding free of their sheaths as he kneaded the air. Hugh hastily finished his sausages, grabbed the dian-stane from its resting place under the chair, and hurried out the back door.

The sound of a bubbly purring exhaust brought him around the low wall to an alley between the rose bushes. This opened to a clear gravel space, in which crouched a 1974 Jaguar E-Type roadster. Hugh gawked for a moment at the machine that he truly did not expect to see here. Just because his truck was a simple, salt-rusted clunker in no way meant that he was incapable of recognizing a classic when he saw it. Nonetheless, it did strike him as out of place for Hulda to own such a rarity. She sat in the driver's seat, a shining white-gold figure amidst silvery leather upholstery and salt-slicked moonglow metal. The car was a uniform grey that emphasized the fluid lines of the body style; coming around its front, Hugh noted that even though the chrome grille was dulled by age and exposure its characteristic Cheshire-cat grin was undaunted by the rust that had turned all the shiny parts of his truck a lackluster brown.

"I'd honestly expected us to walk to Yetnasteen or ride goats there or be whisked away on the wind, or something else primitive and magical," Hugh babbled as he opened the left door. He got in under Hulda's amused gaze.

"There is no need to spend the extra energy and time that such travel methods would require," she replied. A light rain began to tap on the windscreen as she backed the car down the drive and pulled away northbound on the B9064. The pattering precipitation's rhythm quickened on the hardtop while they cruised up the road.

"Your Finman and Nuggle bend the rules of the world at will because they are born of that energy. The use of it taxes them, but not as greatly as it taxes those who are merely bound to it. Spae-wives, stone guardians, magicians, witches, call us what you may, we are but weavers. We take hold of the threads and strands of life and we alter their paths, sometimes for wondrous good and sometimes to breathtaking ill. Whatever the outcome, your goal should always be balance. Life recovers from amazing wounds and pitfalls, but play that energy out of balance and you can break that tenacity into chaos. That also means learning when to interfere and when to take your hands off the strands. All things in time, Hugh Reid."

"Kellbrue said I'm a finman," Hugh admitted, muttering barely loudly enough to be heard over the grey Jaguar's growling engine. "But I don't-"

"All the more reason for caution, Hugh Reid. You will find yourself to be capable of great feats, but always remember that the risks you take affect more than just yourself. You always sow what you reap."

The road curved, then widened briefly. Hulda carried through the curve into a parking area. She brought the Jaguar to a stop, informing Hugh, "We walk from here."

Getting out of the car, Hugh couldn't spot their target standing stone. He shrugged, willing to assume that Hulda knew what she was doing. However, the way she left the car running made him wonder.

"Will it be alright to leave it with the keys in?" He questioned when she shut the door.

"Hm? Oh, yes, he's perfectly comfortable here. Come, the track is there." Despite the odd reply Hugh followed as Hulda lead the way to a hard-packed carriage path. They passed the Faraclett Head sign, keeping a post-and-wire pasture fence on their left. Within minutes the gentle angle of the track gave way to a straight, and up ahead he spotted it. Away to the east the waters of the Loch of Scockness sparkled, but just behind the fence ahead a beefy seven-foot-tall stone stood silent sentry. Moss and lichen - green and orange like a wistful representative of Irish unity - decorated its grey head. The Yetnasteen stood at the bottom of a hill amidst eager daffodil stalks in the shadow of a flock of sheep that grazed the hillside. Under Hulda's touch the lock chaining the aluminum gate fell away and the gate opened to allow them access.

"Normally," Hulda mused as she closed the gate behind them to prevent the sheep's unauthorized wandering, "There are more visitors here. The land is owned by a farmer, and I paid him a visit a few days ago to bid him make certain that we would be alone. He agreed, though I am happy that he also remembered. We shall not be disturbed."

"A few days ago?" Hugh echoed, confused. "I only arrived last night."

"I have known you were coming for a week, Hugh Reid. Never do I throw runes for myself, but some things have a way of making their truths known. See the crack down the side here? That is where our giant's forearms and shins are tucked together. He sits curled like a baby, hands covering his face in a childish attempt to hide from the light. Every new year he is permitted to go to the loch and drink, provided he returns to this place. Every year he agrees to this binding, and so he is alive. He hears us; he knows you are here, though not yet why. Time's passing is nothing to him in the stone. Coward though he is, simple though he is, do not deny his strength. He is mighty, and he is angered by my words. When I release him, you must focus all your desires on his return to this stone-bound state. He must not flee. Fix him in your mind as you see him now, and remind him of his oath of being. If you do this correctly, the dian-stane will cause your intention and desire to be truth. Do you have any questions?"

"What if I fail?" Hugh gasped, trembling. "I've never done anything like this before! How do I know I'll do it right?"

"None of us have done anything before until we try."

"Can't we practice on something first? A bird? A piece of grass?"

Hulda smirked, shaking her head. "Birds and grass are not under an oath of stone-binding. It is this giant or nothing. And if you choose nothing-"

"I know: eternal winter. I got that ultimatum already," Hugh summated glumly.

"Well then, prepare yourself. Rid your thoughts of doubt and focus on the giant as he is now." She turned from Hugh and raised her hands toward Yetnasteen. "Devourer, I command you, rise!"

A thunderous blast shook the earth, and the crack in the stone widened with a wind-sheer roar.

CHAPTER TEN

The way Yetnasteen unfolded was captivating and terrifying all at once. Overhead, the fleece-grey clouds drew in at breathtaking speed. Was that bluster thunder howling, or the stone-skin breaking? Hugh feared it might be both, and staggered back some steps as the time-worn stone before him took to its feet. The haggard mouth of the giant sneered vengefully, cracked lips revealing jagged yellow teeth. He cried out, "Why would I flee from you, puny witch?!"

Flea-black eyes were screwed in hate toward Hulda - Hugh wondered, cautiously, whether Yetnasteen even saw him at all. And the spae-wife; well, Hugh was astonished. She stood defiantly, corn-yellow hair whipping in the circling winds, blue eyes shining with a maniacal exhilaration. Her white clothes and white flesh seemed almost to glow white-hot like star fire, like permafrost; her pale lips parted with a ferocious, wildly gleeful shout - and, very abruptly, the wheeling sky came to heel. The spiraling clouds wrenched to such a sudden calm that it was almost comical; Hugh could just imagine the universe bending its ear to its master like a mastiff at the gate.

"Because, Devourer, you know who I am!" She hollered, and when he reached grasping digits toward her a brilliant light flared from her unearthly glow. The giant reeled away from the light, moaning as though singed.

Keeping her gaze on the giant, Hulda bestirred Hugh with a call to action. "Now, Warden! Remember Yetnasteen as he was, locked in his skin of stone, and return him to rock!"

Without any clear idea of how to make that happen, Hugh lifted his dian-stane between himself and the seeking giant. Hulda's evocation had pointed out his existence to the jotun. Pit-black eyes squinted as Yetnasteen searched for him, and Hugh knew his time was up when the giant hummed victoriously.

"You brought a friend, witch! He does not shine like you. I will break his bones instead and bury you both!" Roared the Jotun.

Hugh squeaked despite his resolve for a good show, and, hands shaking, stared the giant down through the hole in the dian-stane's middle. He set his thoughts fiercely on the memory of the humble, moss-covered standing stone. The dian-stane warmed in his grip, growing hotter as Hugh tried to mentally push that memory-image onto the reality before him. And - wonder beyond wonders - something actually happened.

Yetnasteen stumbled in his charge toward Hugh, impacting the ground hard on his knee. Spitting rage, he reared back to see that his left foot and ankle had hardened into anchoring rock, and the effect was creeping up his leg. The giant laid his hand on the casing and under his touch it reversed, restoring his former mobility.

"Fie, Warden! Not quick enough," shouted Hulda. Even as Yetnasteen lunged again toward Hugh, the spae-wife split the clouds with a gesture and a foreign word. Sunlight dashed through the opening, bathing the giant and the hillside. The Jotun, stone-skinned, hit the ground face-first at Hugh's feet. He felt the landing in his heart, which was beating faster than Hugh would have believed possible. But it wasn't all terror and adrenaline from the assault - that little working of magic had awakened something else in him: euphoria. He'd felt the edge of it briefly when the giant's foot had turned to stone, and the afterglow kept him rooted as Hulda pushed his chest. She struck his face hard with an open palm, bringing him red-cheeked out of the stunning sensation.

Of course, Hulda recognized what he was going through. She'd woken others to magic before, though never under such dire urgency. But what she'd done to Yetnasteen was not the full binding. Depending entirely on the unbridled sun to keep him trapped, there was no time to revel in Hugh's awakening. It must wait for his ultimate success, or there would be nothing worth celebrating.

"Ow!" Declared Hugh, rubbing his cheek. "What? I got his foot, didn't I?"

"Oh, aye, for half a breath you got his foot. But giants work with decay, Warden, and entropy. Anything you can create he can break. It must be all at once and it must be fast if you are to stop him."

"Well, how? I focused on how he looked when we arrived, just like you said."

"That may be so, but you did not remind him of his stone-bound oath. That is the binding, and the power is in you, in the stone, and in the words." She counted the three with raised fingers as she described them.

"All three must be for sound stone skin to take all, strong and unbroken, and stay stone-strong 'til his drink night."

Yetnasteen growled, or maybe it was the rock cracking as he struggled. Hulda glanced to the sky, where the clouds were knitting back together. "He is, even now, resisting me. See how he draws the moisture away, look!" The earth below his prone body was parched, the daffodils shriveling. "How mundane," Hulda smirked.

Hugh wondered at her calm, and then realized what it meant. "He's creating cloud cover!" The fisherman exclaimed.

"Yes, Warden. By desecrating the life here, depriving the plants and wee creatures of precious water, he humidifies the air. It is an excess, and nature is out of balance, so the moisture collects high above and forms clouds. It is slow magic, subtle death, but then so is time. And if there is anything Yetnasteen is familiar with, it is time. Move away," she bade Hugh as the sunlight diminished and the grey stone warmed to flesh tones.

He stumbled back just in time to see the giant's feet slide and his knees plough the ground. Ignoring the dirt on his forehead and nose, Yetnasteen rose once more and sought his adversaries.

"You cannot trap me any longer, puny witch!" He taunted. "Decay never dies; it only grows. It consumes all, and the cycle turns. The night of the Jotun has returned; the long winter has begun. My frost cousins have freed Teran of the Mither's chains, and for it we are given a world without sunlight! Ah - there you are!"

He had spotted Hugh, who was thinking hard about his task. Invigorated by Hulda's advice and his near victory, Hugh lifted the dian-stane and peered through its central hole, sighting Yetnasteen like a hunter spies his prey with a scope. It was instinctive, and the increasing warmth of the dian-stane encouraged him.

Feeling a little self-conscious about the words he was about to shout, Hugh nonetheless pushed through. He mentally envisioned Yetnasteen as he'd first seen him from the track, and focused that memory through the dian-stane. Just as Yetnasteen found him, Hugh proclaimed, "Devourer, I remind you of your stone-bound oath!"

The giant staggered mid-charge, curling in on himself as though struck by sudden stomach pains. Delighted by his perceived success, Hugh whooped aloud. But something wasn't quite right; Yetnasteen slowly raised his head, hateful eyes narrowed in agonized, blind rage.

"Do not allow doubt in your soul, Warden!" Hulda's voice came to him on a sudden whirl of wind. Looking around, Hugh couldn't find her, but he heeded her words regardless. Hugh steeled his focus on Yetnasteen. He took a deep breath, squashing his second-guesses, and affirmed to himself that this would work. He could do this thing. He was a Rousay Reid!

Fired up and with a liquid quickening in his blood, Hugh roared, "Devourer, I remind you of your stone-bound oath! By this dian-stane I command you, return to your sworn shape!" A cool pressure eased his nerves, plugging his ears and spreading with a heady rush across his entire body. Every hair on his flesh bristled in its wake. It left him electrified.

There in the valley of the hills, the giant bowed. His limbs tucked together, hands covering his face, and in the shadow of the clouds a wave of scaly grey overtook him. And there stood Yetnasteen, the cracked Giant Stone, silently screaming his frustration.

Hugh wobbled, sitting down hard in the grass as the euphoria left him and utter exhaustion took over. He groaned, peeling a hand off the dian-stane and pressing his knuckles over his eyes. A pounding headache pulsed between his temples, swelling and fading and swelling like the pattern of the ocean. Something soft brushed his ear and he twitched aside reflexively. Lifting his hand, Hugh was astonished to see a sleek falcon finish its turn past him, flapping up to the top of Yetnasteen. Talons reached out, wings and tail flared gracefully, and the petite hunter landed purposefully atop the Giant Stone's crown. She turned back around to face Hugh, and as she did her plumes lengthened, body morphing in a strangely beautiful way. Hugh was transfixed as feathers became flesh, wings became blouse and skirt, and the falcon was replaced by the spae-wife Hulda. The golden-haired witch sat victoriously atop Yetnasteen, laughing aloud. Despite his awe Hugh smirked in the wake of her laughter, and his tense fatigue loosened. He couldn't say what the joke was, but maybe it was magic. Changing the normal way of the world was a pretty fine game.

CHAPTER ELEVEN

The rain returned during their drive back to Hulda's cottage. Hugh looked out at the ocean, evaluating it with a professional fisherman's eye. "It's a good day to be a tern," he commented quietly.

"Or a frog," Hulda remarked. She guided the grey Jaguar gently down the road, barely touching the steering wheel. Mesmerized by the sound of rain bouncing off the roof and by the curtain-shrouded movement of the sea, it took Hugh a few minutes to realize that Hulda had changed course. They were no longer headed for the dry, warm cottage but rather for the western side of Rousay. When Hulda turned left after the post office, Hugh asked, "Where are we going?"

"To meet a friend," she replied, composure holding when the Jaguar's wheels dropped off pavement and onto an old dirt track. The car growled in such a cat-like manner that Hugh twisted to check the back seat for stowaways. He found none.

"I think we're past vagaries," he retorted, facing forward again. "But either way I hope they have lunch ready."

Hulda laughed briefly. "I would not count on it, Hugh Reid. Your breakfast should have been enough to last the day. Magic taxes, but you must learn to measure your stamina too." The vehicle slowed to navigate a tricky part of the track. Continuing, Hulda explained, "To aid in the conquering of Teran you must venture to the ocean floor. And to do that, you must know how to breathe underwater. Your nature as a finman makes you capable of it already, but we go to one who will awaken the knowledge of how."

"Well, that would have been handy when I was a wee lad," Hugh grumbled. "I nearly drowned once, you know. My father and I - well, I suppose he wasn't my father, but he and Mother raised me and they deserve the titles. We were on the Brough of Birsay off Mainland, looking for Goatie Buckies and hermit crabs. We both had some small success and I had carried my catch to the shore to see it swim in the sea. Of course, once I put it in the crab went under some ware. I waded in to the tops of my wellies in search of it, but no luck; it was good as gone. In my childish foolishness, I went further, certain it had just crawled quickly. A wave cut up sideways and knocked me forward off my feet. There wasn't much current that day, but when I surfaced again I was meters out from the shore. I'm a fair swimmer, but my wellies bogged my kicks and it seemed as though every time I tried to catch a breath another wave licked over my head. Every time I tried to yell for help I pulled in a mouthful of water instead. My chest started to burn and I struck out harder, flailing desperately, and a cold, bristly seal's head bumped under my hand. The seal pushed its withers into my armpit to raise my head above the sea. Her flipper hit my back hard and made me cough up the water from my lungs enough to wheeze into a spluttering exchange of gasping and hacking. She even towed me into the shallows, where my father waded out and lifted me from the sea.

"When I told him later about the seal he denied seeing

one." Hugh paused, mulling over a sudden suspicion. "You know," he realized aloud, "I suppose the seal must have been a selkie. All my life I've spat on the old stories, but there's no doubting them now, is there?"

"You're lucky they don't hold a grudge," Hulda commented wryly.

Not certain what to say to that, Hugh silently contemplated the spae-wife. And as he did, he experienced another stroke of intuition that left him mentally breathless.

Confident in his suspicion, Hugh accused Hulda, "You know who the seal was. You knew the entire story; tell me! Who was she?"

"It is not mine to tell, Hugh Reid," objected Hulda quietly.

"Maybe not, but it is mine to know, Hulda...whatever-your-last-name-is." Did she even have one? No matter. The two-name calling seemed to be a trend among the supernatural, and Hugh still didn't think of himself in that way. "I've no one else to ask. So tell me who the seal was, please."

Pulling the car to a spot off the side of the ragged road, Hulda considered his request. Releasing a deep breath, she admitted, "I suppose it won't do any harm. The seal was your sister, Hugh Reid. You know of the changeling man for whom you were switched as an infant? He was meant to be groomed for a life among the finfolk as your sister's husband. Mortally wed, she would remain forever young; forever beautiful; forever

67

powerless. But this was not the future that she desired. She watched over you from afar, always close but never near enough to be discovered. That is, until the day the sea tried to claim your life. Your sister was nearby in your hour of need, and it may yet be seen that we have the world to thank her for.

"But such choices have repercussions, and when Death comes to collect it never leaves empty-handed. The human changeling boy was walking on the shore of Hether Blether, looking for his dear seal-lady friend. The raging waves leapt up from nothing, sweeping him underwater before any of the finfolk could stop it. Selkies, bade by your father, rushed to his rescue, but there was no saving him. The current pressed his frail mortal body amidst the stones, crushing the air from his lungs and the light from his eyes. One life promised, and another taken instead. The fates knew one of the two strands would be cut that day, but they spoke naught of it 'til his life was ended."

"If this is all foretold, then what's the point?" Hugh blurted out. The revelation of his sister and her involvement in an attempt on his life had flustered him.

"Were you not listening, Hugh Reid? Yes, some things are fated to occur. But how they come to pass, and when, and where; the details are rarely defined. There is much that we yet control."

Her words calmed him enough for his normally resilient composure to take hold again. There was one more detail worrying at his mind, however, and Hugh gave voice to it. "If that's so, then the fates foretold this

Vore Tullye. Did they say how it would end?"

Hulda smiled, and its hopeful radiance warmed courage into Hugh's soul. "They did not. And that, Hugh Reid, is where you come in."

CHAPTER TWELVE

"And this," Hulda continued, "is where we get out." She opened her door and exited the Jaguar, barely seeming to even notice the rain that immediately dampened her white clothing. Doing his best not to stare at the revealing effect, Hugh followed suit. Hardy though the Orcadian was, he still longed for an umbrella or hat or something to keep the droplets off of his face.

Hugh turned a slow circle to orient himself in the sodden landscape before he caught up with Hulda. "We're just north of Muckle Water," he announced, and realized in a moment of foolishness that that was no surprise to the spae-wife. "There's a smaller pond around here."

"There is," she confirmed. "And it is there, to Peerie Water, that we go. The Nuggle of Muckle Water has agreed to meet us here rather than at its loch. It is a little more private here, and the rain will keep away any who might interrupt us."

"The Nuggle can breathe underwater?" Hugh questioned, remembering the purpose for their detour.

"Indeed. How else do you suppose it manages its trick of luring mortals onto its back and drowning them?"

Conceding, Hugh grumbled, "Aye, a valid point. But I don't remember any gills; how does it work?"

Hulda smirked, and Hugh recognized the expression now. It was the same expression she wore when he was on the verge of stumbling across some secret knowledge. "That is the very thing you are here to discover. Recall,

Hugh Reid, that only a finman may successfully ride a Nuggle. You and the waterhorse are linked on an ancient level. And there it is, waiting by the shore. Why don't you ask it yourself?"

Peering through the precipitation, Hugh eyed the subject of their conversation. It stood as it had on their first meeting, lingering in the shallows up to its fetlocks. Minding his steps on the rain-slick rocks, Hugh wondered if the Nuggle could exit the water fully, or if some portion of it had to remain submerged at all times. Was it more frog or fish?

<FROG, IF YOU MUST KNOW,> boomed a familiar voice in his head. They must have come in range for the Nuggle to hear his thoughts.

"Frog, then," Hugh echoed aloud. His out of place comment roused a curious glance from Hulda. Just as quickly, however, it transitioned to comprehension.

"Ah, so it does speak. I'd always wondered," she murmured.

<ONLY TO FINFOLK,> the Nuggle confirmed smugly in Hugh's mind. Its amused tone was infectious, and Hugh smirked at Hulda. How good it felt to be on the inside of the joke for once!

Quirking a slender brow, Hulda pressed, "What does it say?"

"Oh, nothing of import," Hugh replied with an eye-wrinkling grin. The spae-wife's curious expression darkened toward annoyance, which made Hugh all the more gleeful. He couldn't help but chuckle, such a buzz it was to be the secret holder for a change.

However, Hulda refused to rise to the bait. "No matter, then," she shrugged. Smoothing her scowl back out into her customary half smile, she waved from Hugh to the Nuggle. "We are here for a purpose, Warden. I'm certain our host has other things it could be doing, so let us not waste its time."

<YOU HAVE TOUCHED A NERVE WITH HER, HUGH REID. TREAD CAREFULLY IN THOSE WATERS. THE GODDESS DOES NOT ENJOY BEING MOCKED,> warned the Nuggle.

Its use of the word "goddess" burned some of Hugh's mirth away. He stared hard at the Nuggle, wanting it to clarify. However, he disliked the impulse to ask it aloud, because he had a bitter inkling that this was a mystery Hulda didn't wish for him to discover. If the Nuggle could overhear a mild snoopiness that concerned it, could it pick up on a thought pointed directly at it?

Deciding to try, he focused his gaze at the Nuggle's stern, blue eyes. An odd, constant motion swirled within them; calm, but random, it reminded Hugh of sunlight dancing on dappled water. He peered into that depth, willing his question down it: <WHAT DO YOU MEAN BY GODDESS? KELLBRUE SAID SHE'S A SPAE-WIFE.>

Startled, the Nuggle blinked; an eerie thing to see, as it revealed a secondary frog-like membrane that slid protectively across its eyes. But it nickered approval, ears flicking forward as though to tune in. <VERY GOOD!> Its mental voice was as commending as applause. <ALTHOUGH HARDLY NECESSARY. YOUR SURFACE THOUGHTS ARE CLEAR TO ME. I SUPPOSE SUCH COMMUNICATION WILL WORK OVER DISTANCE, THOUGH, WHEN YOU ARE OUT OF RANGE OF THE PASSIVE EFFECT. NOW, TO THE WORD: KELLBRUE WAS CORRECT, AND SO WAS I. YOU SEE, THE ONE CALLED HULDA IS SIMPLY A CHANNEL. SHE OPENS HERSELF AS A VESSEL FOR POWER, OR KNOWLEDGE, AND THROUGH HER THE SPIRITS AND GODS AND GODDESSES AND ELEMENTS SPEAK. AT PRESENT, AN OLD GODDESS IS AMONG US; HER SHADOW LOOMS BEHIND HULDA, HER EYES SEE THE WORLD THROUGH THE WITCH'S. SHE SEES YOU.>

Hugh's amusement was all departed by now. Cold anxiety took its place as he wondered whether the goddess liked what she saw.

<SHE IS IMPATIENT,> the Nuggle replied, receptive of Hugh's concern. <SO LET US GET ON WITH YOUR INSTRUCTION.> Kneeling to make its height accessible once more, the Nuggle tossed its head over its shoulder as if beckoning him closer. The movement caused the mysterious constant trickle of water in its kelp mane to briefly increase; the soaking strands shed a shower which innocently spattered Hugh. He grimaced, wiping the droplets from his clean-shaven face, and was surprised by the saltiness of it, given the

freshwater loch in which the Nuggle stood.

<CLIMB ON, HUGH REID,> invited the Nuggle. Apprehensive, Hugh hesitated.

"You can't explain it here?"

"There is much to be said for practicum," Hulda argued. "Had you not practiced on Yetnasteen, do you think you'd be ready to face Teran's frost giants?"

His mood now totally soured by that insight, Hugh waded the few steps to stand by the Nuggle.

"Whoever said I'm ready now that I have?" He bemoaned quietly. It was meant to be private, but the Nuggle heard him or picked up on the psychic sentiment. It waited until Hugh grasped its sodden shoulder and swung a leg over its back. Settling with a grunt of exertion, Hugh couldn't quite ignore how cold the damp was becoming now that the grey rain was in effect doubled by his wet mount.

Determined to bring some degree of cheer back into this encounter, no matter how miniscule, the Nuggle encouraged Hugh as it carried him deeper into the middle of the loch. <THAT'S ACTUALLY GOOD,> the waterhorse praised of the fisherman's musings. <FOCUSING ON THE WET IS PART OF THIS. THIS IS A FINFOLK TRICK, ONE PERFECTED BY THE MERMAIDS AND ACCOMPLISHED ONLY TO A POINT OF USEFULNESS BY THE FINMEN. FEEL MY FLESH; HOW IT IS COLD, CLAMMY, SLIPPERY LIKE A FROG'S. THEN YOU MUST THINK OF YOUR OWN SKIN, AND ALLOW IT TO BECOME

THE SAME.>

"What do I do with the dian-stane?"

<NOTHING. IT HAS NO PART IN FINFOLK THINGS. THIS TRICK IS ONE YOUR HEART KNOWS ALREADY - ALL YOU MUST DO IS REMIND YOUR FLESH OF ITS FLUIDNESS.> The Nuggle's mental voice was smug, amused by the pun. <THIS SHOULD BE DEEP ENOUGH.> It announced, slowing to a stop. The water came up to the top of the Nuggle's back, wavelets licking over it with every gust of the rising wind. Its kelp mane sagged in the loch, drifting slowly in the current. <DISMOUNT, HUGH REID. YOU WILL FIND THE DEPTH TO BE SUCH THAT YOU ONLY NEED TO CROUCH AND YOU WILL BE SUBMERGED.>

Thankful that he wouldn't have to tread water with one arm occupied by the dian-stane, Hugh slid into the embrace of the loch. His breath caught briefly as the frigid temperature gripped his chest, but the shock was quick to subside. The mud bottom sucked at his boots, but it was firm enough that he did not fear for his footing. Remaining nearby, the Nuggle's presence provided a sense of safety, and so Hugh closed his eyes and ducked under the surface before he could start overthinking the process.

The last thing he remembered was the fiery tingle on his skin when, like with the giant, he willed it to recall its oath of taking another form. He thought that shivery sensation was the transformation taking hold.

In truth, it was a sudden, rogue lightning bolt that

pierced the waters of the loch, setting them a-boil. The violent, vivid spike struck Hugh directly, and the dian-stane awoke to absorb the energy that should have killed him. It released a massive explosion of searing steam as it was heated by the lightning and cooled immediately in the frigid loch. Beside Hugh, the Nuggle had no such defense. The water passing so freely between its flesh, its very cells, and its environment was hotter than boiling, and the pain of its passing screamed in noiseless agony from its yawning maw. It died, silent and swift.

As the waterhorse's legs buckled, a golden, angelic being scooped her arms under Hugh's. It was Hulda, sprung from the shoreline by a massive pair of grey-plumed falcon wings. Like a valkyrie straight out of legend, she lifted the unconscious fisherman from his boiling bath. Powerful strokes of her wings carried them both back to the shore, where the leaden Jaguar waited with open doors to accept them.

The thunder rolled like booming laughter, peal after peal, as the dusky vehicle sped away in a flurry of mud.

CHAPTER THIRTEEN

Sshk, sshk, rasped the broom's stiff bristles as Hulda dragged them across the moss-flossed pavers. She swept with a methodic rhythm that was almost meditative: not fast but not slow; an even pace that steadily shunned the dust and dirt after the retreating light of civil dusk. The rain had stopped, but the residual damp mucked up the straw and shortened the broom's usefulness in this daily task.

She worked from the stoop down the path to the street, clearing the walk of debris from the day. In the cottage's guest room, Hugh lay in a heavy, dreamless sleep. Sshk, sshk, cawed the broom, and with every stroke Hulda willed a healing prayer for the injured man. Good intentions and hopes of well-being for the Warden filled her thoughts and pumped forth on every sweep as blood is pulled through veins or breath is pressed from lungs. Her effort was hardly necessary, for the dian-stane was doggedly set to the task of repairing its soulmate. Its interference had already saved Hugh's life, and as Hulda swept it hastened the healing of the burns his flesh had suffered in the boiling water.

Hulda smirked, amused by the memory of Hugh's hunger earlier. He would need nothing less than a small feast to replenish the energy used by the dian-stane. The brief moment of wry humor drew a chuckle from the spae-wife, and she raised her head as she dashed the last of the dust into the street, completing her task.

Her smile vanished when she glimpsed a fleeting

motion dart between the spiny roadside rose bushes. Filled suddenly with an inexplicable sense of dread, Hulda retreated swiftly up the path. She flattened her back to the door, one hand holding the broom defensively in front of her while the other scrambled for the knob. Her breaths came shorter and faster, panic mounting as she searched blindly; and finally felt the round knob under her fingers. She gripped it frantically, giving a firm twist and nearly tripping over the threshold in her haste to get inside. Catching her hip with the edge, Hulda slammed the door shut again faster than she'd opened it.

It was dark in the small front room. The space was familiar, though, and Hulda knew it well enough to maneuver in its corners with her eyes closed. However, lingering nerves caused her hand to shake and fumble with the lock. When the bolt finally clicked into place, she let go of the breath she'd been holding and rested her forehead against the door. A few seconds passed, audibly tracked by the ticking movement of the clock. And then, just as Hulda was gathering her strength to move away from the door, the timepiece announced the hour. Freezing mainly on instinct, Hulda mentally counted each chime. One, two, three, four, five, six - it passed the proper time as Hulda feared it would - seven, eight, nine, ten - stop, oh monstrous, stop! - eleven, twelve; thirteen. The final echo faded like a dying scream in her ears, chills tracing its ghost all across her skin. Thirteen strokes: a portent with deadly association.

And then it came. The knock, loud and urgent, pounded thrice against the door. It reverberated eerily in her skull as the vibration passed through the thick timbers where her forehead touched the barrier. Hulda pulled away, stumbling back a step as she pressed her hand over her mouth to keep from shrieking. The knock repeated the same three-strike pattern, and the locked handle creaked and rattled as whatever was outside tried the knob. Overwhelmed by the malevolent energy of the moment, it took all of Hulda's resolve to step forward. Terrified though she may be, she could not shrink away without knowing what evil waited on her stoop. Barely daring to breathe, she stretched to her tiptoes and balanced with her fingertips touching the door to peer through the peephole. Having no guess of what to expect, what she saw tightened her stomach with intense shock.

There was absolutely nothing visible on the other side.

THUD!

Bolting away from the door, Hulda brandished her broom high like a lance and dashed for the stairs. The noise had come from the guest room above, and the howling of the cats pushed all speed to her heels.

CHAPTER FOURTEEN

The guest room door was open and gave Hulda no resistance. With a ready palm she rebounded off the edge of the frame, entering the small space without an interruption to her momentum. Filled with a short chest of drawers, a plush bed just big enough for two to rest comfortably, a small wicker chair by the hearth, and a simple bedside table, the bedroom was full enough already. But now, with a foreign creature coiled atop the chest of drawers, two cats angrily bristled to double their already large size, and the spae-wife in the doorway, it was overly crowded. Hulda noted the open window through which the intruder had undoubtedly entered, although the majority of her attention was absorbed by the out of place creature.

"Fachin!" She hissed, and instantly became the focus of its singular eye. "You're far from home, devil!" The one-eyed, one-armed, one-legged monster was known to live on the highest peaks of the Scottish mountains, and had never before ranged as far as the Orkney Islands. Its presence here - now - was more disturbing for Hulda than even its legendary grotesque appearance.

The Scottish faerie split its wide mouth in a cruel sneer. "True, spae-wife!" It declared, voice rough like death's own rattle. "The balance is thrown and the veil thinned, or have ye nae felt it? In the small hours and the glaring civil dusk I am free tae roam where I please. Even under my fur," he stroked his hairy chest, "the bitter cold creeps. Mayhaps I shall find a warmer place tae stay. But right here, right now, I am to act on another's full petition.

The pride to be so required! The Fachin is never requested, nor summoned, only denied. Feared! What is to fear but adversity? Horror! See - it is so vile, so malformed!"

It twisted where it crouched, writhing under the lick of its own whip-words. "Beast! Blight! Not so, but who will hear the words spoken true of heart but foul in the eye?" It sneered, drawing a deep breath into its withered frame. Mesmerized by the vehemence of its rant, mangled though its words were, Hulda bestirred as the Fachin's shadow seemed to swell along with its mane. The blue-black feathers that fleeced its neck and crown ruffled into a mighty, iridescent crest when its single eye focused again on the man prone on the bed.

"But now," the Fachin moaned, low and guttural like liquid lead, "to it!" Its voice wound up in the span of those two words into a brittle screech. Flattening its plumes flush, the Fachin coiled down on its single leg, then sprang from the chest of drawers. It lunged in a beautifully vicious inky bolt toward Hugh, solitary hand stretched for his vulnerable neck. Black-nailed, cracked fingers hooked like claws for his jugular. Hulda was at once affronted twicefold: first because of its audacity to attack a guest in her home, and second because of the poison that must have beguiled it onto this path of murder. Though the Fachin was known for an occasional destructive bent, she'd never before heard of one that sought to shorten a man's life. All cases of death associated with it were by coincident: heart attacks born of the terror inspired in a mortal's soul at the sight of the misshapen beast.

Before she could react, however, the tabby and the tomcat moved as one. The striped feline launched straight for the Fachin's cyclops eye, filling its vision with raw, spitting indignation and causing it to cry out in surprise. Routed from its original intent, the Fachin flailed its solitary arm to try to bat the assailant out of its way. Its defense was spoiled by the grey tomcat, however, who had aimed his flight slightly higher than the tabby. The bear-like cat sailed energetically over the Fachin's feathered head, rotating his body with a fluid flick of his hindquarters and tail. He twisted in midair, bringing his fore and aft claws to bear. The bite of his talons sank deeply into the neck, skull and shoulders of the Fachin, plunged firmly by the sheer weight of his landing. Needle-sharp fangs penetrated the protective plumage, nipping furiously into the Fachin's nape. Driven mad by the pain it thrust its arm back over its shoulder, crooked nails pursuing a grip to disengage the feline.

And then the tabby was on the Fachin's face, toe-barbs mangling its eye, lips, nose and breastbone. The invader screamed, a haunting keen full of agony and frustration. Its attack successfully interrupted, it hit the floorboards beside the bed and rolled, contorting limbs and body as it attempted to free itself of its enemies. One at a time, the tomcat and the tabby unfastened from their prey, backing off to the corners of the room. Freed, the Fachin hauled itself stiffly upright; only to be met by Hulda. She kept it on the floor kneeling in supplication before her with a simple touch of her broomstick, brandished so that the iron cap on the butt of the handle hovered a threatening millimeter from the Fachin's forehead.

Fury burned in its broken gaze, and it whined, "Begone, witch, so I may complete my task and begone myself! The window is small and soon I will be trapped. My freedom hinges on the Warden's death and I will have them both!"

"You'll have disappointment, then, Fachin. Get thee back to the bristlecone mountains and enjoy the rest of your eternity in peace. But come 'round here again and you'll not find mercy a second time. Go lick your wounds and remember your place." Hulda commanded sternly.

"No! The task must be completed!" It howled plaintively.

What threat had been made to make it behave so? Maybe none - maybe the offer of freedom from its solitary haunt was sweet enough when coupled with the tainted honey of a reminder of the revulsion caused in mortals by the sight of its monstrous form. How better to get a dimmer mind to destroy the world than to embellish the lack of love the world had for its pitiable soul? Regardless of its motivation, Hulda could not allow its victory.

"Begone! Back to whence you came. Fachin, begone!" She compelled it and pressed the cold-forged iron cap to its flesh. The touch sizzled and burned, branding the faerie creature with its kiss, and the Fachin folded in on itself before disappearing with a silent pop. The implosion was absent of sound, but the resulting pressure in Hulda's ears created the echoing illusion.

Turning to check on the prone man, Hulda noticed
that the shadows had indeed lengthened. The time of civil
dusk had come to a close for another day. Another minute
more and she would not have been able to simply return
the Fachin down the route it had come. She would have
truly had to banish it, or incapacitate it another way. A
more chilling thought followed: if the veil was so thinned,
so compromised by this conflict, was the Fachin just the
first of many invasions to come? Would they be faced
with trespassers every evening until Teran was once again
secured firmly in his springtime bonds?

A cold certainty settled in her gut: yes, that was the
way of it. The tide was rising, and if they did not resolve
this soon they would all be swept to the depths.

Easing her hip down onto the edge of the bed, Hulda
rested the broom's bristles on the floor. The tomcat and
the tabby rejoined her, alighting on the covers and each
tucking limbs and tails in so that they laid like furry loaves
across Hugh's legs. The spae-wife shivered, though not
for cold, as she observed the faint glow of the dian-stane
clutched to Hugh's chest. His burns were almost healed,
and by morning she was certain that he would be fully
recovered and ravenous.

And then - would he be ready? The recent events
proved to Hulda that they were truly running out of time.
She needed the finman, the Warden of the Stone. But was
the fisherman prepared for that mantle?

Time would tell. She had done what she could to open
his eyes and his channels, and now it came down to what

he would do with it all. The evening breeze brushed the curtains aside, freshening the room with a foreboding coolness. Its chill carried the bite of hoarfrost, the whisper of winter. Fearing that it might be some new attack, a tendril of Teran's influence reaching out on the trail of the Fachin's retreat, Hulda rose to close the window. She was stopped, however, by movement on the bed. Hugh's eyes were open, face turned to observe her.

He smiled ever so slightly when she hesitated, and spoke through barely parted lips: "Don't. The wind is mine - it's hot in here. Where...?"

"You're safe; back at my cottage," Hulda answered, finishing somewhat lamely. Aye, he was safe, at least just for now. There were plenty of things that lurked just past the veil of darkness, watching and waiting. But Hulda's worries were eased as Hugh's eyes closed again to return to his healing repose; eyes that, when open, had been filled with the black, liquid depth of the sea. The Mither's warmth made those jet chips into molten obsidian, and his voice, hoarse though it was from injury and lack of use, was strong. If the Mither o' the Sea was with him now, then the evaluation was beginning. She would see him as he was, measure the thread of his potential, and hopefully would claim him as her own. For there were few beings in the world more precious to the Mither o' the Sea than the finfolk.

Hulda returned to her seat on the edge of the bed, to remain there as Hugh's breathing evened out into the cadence of the dreamer. She knew the goddess who guided that dream, and ever so quietly Hulda suffered the acid of jealousy. What would she show him; what secrets would she reveal? This one was not for her knowing, and with a sigh Hulda came to terms with that. After all, though the silver glow of moonlight could reveal wonders, so too did it hide the horrors of the dark.

CHAPTER FIFTEEN

Fog prevailed. Hugh could tell he was on a beach strictly because of the damp spray of the salty air and the sound of the waves dragging over the small stones which, piled, composed the terrain underfoot. No matter how hard he squinted or rubbed at his eyes he couldn't see more than a meter past the toe of his boots. So he stood still, listening inward to the way the swell and ebb of the tide matched the pulse drumming between his ears. It was excruciatingly peaceful, and he felt calm in a way he hadn't in years. Maybe in his entire life. Deep in the pit of his gnawing stomach he knew there was something terrible impending that he ought to be white-knuckled with stress over, but every time he tried to focus on the problem the rhythm of the sea called him back to serenity. Ever since the storm that had tossed his boat ashore and since the trow that had appeared in his house, Hugh felt as though his life had been shifted into a frantic pace. It was a treat to take a moment of tranquility to just breathe.

He knew the moment was over when the heat of his brow became enough that he noticed it through the cool, enveloping seaspray. With a spiral too beautiful for words, the mist began to clear. An inexplicable sadness gently stroked his heart in its absence. However, his sight was restored, and what it revealed was just as astonishing.

Green. There was so much green. Growing things of every variety filled the scenery except for the thin strip of rocky shore where the land transformed into the sea. A distant sound alerted him to the presence of cattle, its belligerent call answered by another in close proximity.

As the last of the mist cleared its obscuring banks were replaced by the warming glow of the summer sun. Golden light played over the bobbing barley, the curl-clad corn. It danced - liquid gold and emerald - in the gem-bright streams which meandered through the landscape. Hugh could not see all of these things from where he stood on the coast, but he knew - everything from the smell of the sunlight, the taste of the abundant warmth, the soul-sensitive touch of plants thriving and animals coexisting, the pure calm of harmony shielded by the tide's surrounding roosts - something deep in a memory but not his remembered this place.

"Hildaland," spoke a voice sweet and sunny like blueberry mead. He heard it in its silence in the circumnavigating breeze and in the space between his ears where the Nuggle had spoken to him. And he knew - it made sense didn't it? - that the being speaking to him now was the Mither o' the Sea. All seamen knew her voice, whether they admitted it or not. While he had denied it all his life before, Hugh was well past that now. This sense of hearing was different from the Nuggle's purely psychic projections, Hugh realized. Her words were expressed in the world around him and translated in his mind simultaneously.

"Correct on all accounts, Hugh Reid," the Mither o' the Sea confirmed. He hoped he wasn't imagining the pride in the caress of the breeze on his cheek.

"You named this place Hildaland, but that can't be," Hugh declared aloud, certain the goddess would hear him nonetheless. "Hildaland was occupied long ago and renamed Eynhallow, and then abandoned after an illness culled the people. There are no signs of that civilization here."

A cow produced her deep hailing again as though to argue his point, but the Mither o' the Sea spoke through it instead. "Those things happened, but all the same this is Hildaland. You see the island as it was, not as it is. Once this verdant place was the summer home of the Finfolk, before the iron religion of man displaced them to Hether Blether. This is why it is familiar to you, Hugh Reid. The magic in your blood and the memory in your soul remember this place for once, long ago, your people dwelled here during long, prosperous summers."

"Then you've taken me back in time?" Hugh questioned, trying to wrap his head around what was happening.

"Not quite. This is a dream, Hugh Reid. Your body lies in the spae-wife's cottage still. Your spirit, however, is here with me, connected to your body by its fate-thread. Fear not, however, for Hulda watches over it. For another night and another day, you are safe."

"And then?"

"The civil dusk will join the worlds and Teran's minions will tear through. This assault will not be as gentle as the first; there will be damage." Her voice was woeful in its kindness as she mourned something not yet lost.

"What damage?" Pressed Hugh. "Death? Injury?"

"No, Hugh Reid, it cannot be said. That is only one path among many. We are at a crossroads now, and the turning point is nigh. Teran prepared well this winter and resists me even at the height of my power because, down on the bottom of the sea, he has called in help. He has summoned the ancient titans from their frozen land of Jotunheim, and committed them to breaking my restraints which have always worked to hold him. We cannot go on pulling at the world so, and my strength has begun to fail."

"Can you show him to me?" It was a shot in the dark, but Hugh thought if he could get a glimpse of what they were dealing with maybe he could pass it on to Hulda. Surely she would know what to do if she knew what they faced.

The scenery abruptly changed. All across the landscape, the lush crops shrivelled. "No, Hugh Reid. To do that would be to show him your soul, and that is a critically foolish idea."

Death keens chilled him as the herd of cattle dropped to the ground, knees breaking as the life drained from their plump frames. The voice continued, "Instead, I will show you the power of his attendants, and what awaits if they succeed."

The sunlight dimmed to the grey half-light of a winter midday, and snow began to drift from above. Green ground-covers faded to the dry, crackling brown of lifeless surrender, and were quickly hidden from view by the thick snow piles. A world once multi-hued became monochromatic. And cold - so cold, it made his bones ache and burned in his lungs. Skeletal ribs curled like claws from the cow corpses' icey berths, and a raven circled down to land upon one's barren tip. He stretched his neck, feathers rattling tall, and croaked an echoing cry. It was answered by howls; the wolf-calls rolled in from all sides, and above and below, bounding over the frozen island like frolicking ghosts. Frothing as far as the eye could see, the ocean roiled and roared, lunging upon the shore with more wind-whipped fury than Hugh had ever seen in all his years working the water. Spreading its death -angel's wings, the raven took flight. It turned low over the landscape, then with one more lonesome squawk it abandoned the land to voyage over the sea.

Casting a solitary shadow in the muted light, Hugh contemplated the frozen island, bereft of all other life and thus soul-shatteringly terrible. In a clean, pristine way, though, it was also magnificent.

"For now," agreed the Mither o' the Sea. Hugh was not surprised that she could sense his emotions. "But without the cycle of the season, this is where it ends. A short visit to the land of death is breathtaking in its allure. But by its very being, one cannot live here. There is no rebirth, no renewal, no progression. There is no tomorrow."

Inspired by the pessimism, Hugh mused aloud, "Everything dies anyway, given enough time. So what's the point of prolonging this? All we do is spare millions of lives from suffering."

"That may be so, Hugh Reid, but we do more than

that. We may deny the world from experiencing hardship, but so too do we deny all its creatures and beings from experiencing wonder. Death is meaningless without having lived to reach it. Loneliness is made bearable by the memory of the joys had. Pain is made bearable because of the basic trust in the cycle; because of the hopeful confidence that though there is hurt now there will again be pleasure, and awe, and excitement. And that, if nothing else, is the meaning of life: to live, to experience all one can so that when the end comes it can be embraced knowing that it is not the only journey in the world; it is merely the last. You see this frozen stop as magnificent because you know that somewhere beneath its empty crust there is life or beauty or wonder growing, and the desolation cannot last forever. It is hope for a moment of renewal that makes a moment of decay lovely, and see: you are right!"

The grey sky above burst suddenly with color. Burning great swaths of spring-green, summer-gold, autumn-red and winter-blue flourished overhead. They mingled, separated, blended and intensified, dancing from pole to pole and filling his sight. It was the most impressive display of the aurora ever presented, and in his heart Hugh knew this was because it was the stark opposite of what he'd just witnessed.

He wiped his knuckle across his eyes, shedding tears that he hadn't realized had sprung there.

The Mither o' the Sea's voice whispered in the fall of those salty droplets. "This is why we fight. This is why the cycle must be allowed to continue."

"I understand," Hugh breathed.

"I know."

The hues of the aurora exploded, raining down upon the island like glittering stars. As they settled, the snow and ice melted away. Green life stretched from the soil, and something shifted the earth between Hugh's feet. Looking down, he watched the smallest sea turtle dig out from its buried egg. Soft flippers pedaling, it drove headlong in the instinctive dash for the sea. A gull arrived, striking like lightning for the tender morsel, but it was foiled as the waves welcomed the tiny life. Bemoaning its misfortune, the seabird wheeled high, drawing Hugh's eye with it. The island was restored to its summer splendor. Cattle grazed once more on the edges of the fields, and sunlight gleamed golden in the tops of the crops. The peace of plenty warmed him, and Hugh savored it with the knowledge that it would eventually end.

"Hildaland has ended," the Mither o' the Sea reminded him. "But it has also been renewed. Each time things change, but even in that there is beauty, for if each turn of the cycle was the same then there would be nothing new to enjoy. There are many great deaths in what Teran seeks to achieve, and that indeed is one of them."

The mist began to creep in off the ocean. "Now, carry this message to Hulda for me. She will be displeased that it does not come directly, but I must reserve my strength for what is to come.

Tell her this, and tell her true.

Ice stands with winter below.

The sea summoned the mountain and hides from her True Seeming.

Vengefully she guards him, seeing in his place another."

Knitting quickly together, the mists' tendrils swiftly enveloped the island; or maybe it wrapped woolly around Hugh, but either way he was soon shrouded again in its embrace.

In the beating of the blood in his head, the Mither o' the Sea bid Hugh farewell. "It is time to awaken, Hugh Reid. Indeed, it is time to rise up, for time is running out. Remember the words, and retell them exactly."

He wanted to assure her that he would remember, but his chest was under a lot of pressure. Hugh couldn't draw in enough breath to speak, and he began to panic as his vision darkened. He struggled, breathing in deeply and quickly, but no use; something heavy was preventing him from filling his lungs. Finally he swung his arm to dislodge it, and felt something soft and furry.

Snapped awake by the touch, Hugh found himself face to face with the tabby tiger cub. Bright green eyes stared back at his startled gaze. The feline was curled atop the dian-stane, whose healing heat was no longer needed and was now slowly fading. Displeased that its cozy warming pad was no longer active, the tabby slowly rose. It arched its back, stretching every muscle all at once, from ears to toes to twitching tail. Then it casually blinked at Hugh before walking leisurely to the end of the bed. There an effortless jump placed it atop the chest of drawers, where it settled on its haunches. Tail coming around to drape over it paws, the feline announced Hugh's awakening with a yawning, "Mrow!"

Hulda jerked awake. She had moved to the chair and fallen asleep during her vigil. Reacting defensively at first, she gripped the broomstick firmly. Once she saw that all was quiet and Hugh's eyes were open and restored to normal, she relaxed and crossed to the bed.

"Well?" She queried, somewhat abruptly.

"I'm feeling much better, thanks," Hugh replied, tone brusque from the rudeness.

"There's no time for niceties, Hugh Reid. I can see perfectly well that you're recovered. Did the Mither o' the Sea give you a message?"

He shouldn't have been surprised, but Hugh was still impressed that she assumed. "She did, as a matter of fact."

When it was clear that he was baiting her to ask, Hulda ground her teeth but gave him his moment. "Alright, O Warden of the Stone, would you please do me the honor of sharing it?"

Grinning ear to ear, Hugh acquiesced. His voice even shared the same cadence in which the words had been given to him:

"Tell her this, and tell her true.

Ice stands with winter below.

The sea summoned the mountain and hides from her True Seeming.

Vengefully she guards him, seeing in his place another."

He paused, watching Hulda's face carefully as she adopted a contemplative expression. "She seemed fairly certain that you'd know what it meant."

Hesitating, Hulda slowly replied, "Yes, it is one of the clearest foretellings she's given me. But its meaning is troublesome. If it is true, and it must be, then Teran has crossed some serious boundaries in his quest." She trailed off, thinking hard on the challenge ahead.

Stirring, Hugh eased off the bed, popping what seemed like every joint in his body in the effort. "Well, while you do that, I need a piss and a feast."

"There's a lamb stew warming on the stove," Hulda supplied, certain that he would find everything he needed. She sat on the bed, warmed by his recent repose, and stroked the tabby who leaped to join her. Hulda crooked a finger to scratch the feline's chin. "He's playing with more power than I thought," she muttered. "But then, so are we."

CHAPTER SIXTEEN

When Hulda made her way downstairs, she was greeted by the sight of Hugh setting the last dish into the drying rack. He'd done all the washing up and set aside a bowl of the stew, which he quickly explained, "That's for you; I'd guessed you hadn't eaten yet."

Touched by the gesture, Hulda thanked him and carried the bowl delicately to the table. The cats swarmed around her ankles, their dazzling eyes studying every movement of her spoon. Hulda was surprised that they weren't on the table itself, for they were usually bolder than this with food, until she spotted the dian-stane across from her. The cats almost seemed to be giving it a respectful amount of space. She smirked, amused by the idea.

Pre-dawn light slowly glazed the sky, filtering through the leaden window over the sink. Hulda could see that clouds were gathering in the distance already, heralding yet another storm to come.

Deep in the depths of the ocean,

down on the dark ocean floor,

cracks torn clean in the solid rock let lava-blood outpour.

There in the fallow flagstones fracture

under friction's flowing flesh

and trap the god of winter in a sizzling, core-hot

mesh.

> Teran rages, rants and roars
>
> but still the bonds hold true
>
> but for the sides where his giants' frost manage to sunder through.
>
> Then the huntress golden-clad
>
> strikes with her hunting knife
>
> to pry the old god free by the power of her strife.
>
> 'Tis not Teran that her eyes see
>
> but the visage of another.
>
> In winter's stead her vision red
>
> holds Njord, her sea-born lover.
>
> So stricken Skadi was summoned down
>
> from her mountain nest on high
>
> to fight to free
>
> -what treason be!-
>
> tricked by a Seeming lie.

"Take your paws off me, ya overgrown trout, I'm going aren't I!"

"Aye, you are, and you'll keep going until we're there!"

The exchange happening outside the cottage quickly attracted all its inhabitants' attentions. Hulda stared hard at the grey tomcat, which abandoned its breakfast begging to trot for the door. Exiting through a flap that seemed barely big enough, it went to investigate.

Outside in the road, the conversation continued.

"Well, it's just an old ruin, see? Ya dragged me all this way for nought."

"It's under a Seeming, you dark-dwelling dolt. If you're uncomfortable I'm not sorry, because he was in your howe and you should have given it back then. It's not right, and you know it."

"'Twas for his own good. Keep him out of the sea and keep him hidden. If your father told you about him coming to Hether Blether then he surely told you the rest of it!"

"Aye, he did, after much convincing. And how well did that plan work? He became a fisherman!"

"That's not a rare occupation to find in the Orkney Islands, lass."

Hugh quirked a brow at Hulda. "One of them is Kellbrue," he identified in a whisper. "The other is female, and familiar."

Seeing his confusion, Hulda nodded. "Of course your ears remember it. No amount of time can make one forget the sound of a family member's voice. It is your sister, Hugh Reid."

Hugh nearly tripped over his own feet in his haste to rush the door. So eager was he to meet his childhood savior that he went without sparing a second thought for the dian-stane. It was left lying on the table, and Hulda smirked at it before she followed in his wake.

Flinging the door open, Hugh leapt onto the stoop. At first, he only saw the front garden and the hedge of rose bushes, and over them the pastures and the ever-present ocean. But then he glimpsed a swaying grey snake at the edge of the roses; no, the tip of the tomcat's tail. They must be on the other side! He clattered barefoot down the stone path and rounded the corner of the hedge.

There at the side of the B9064 a woman was bent at the waist, fully engrossed with petting Hulda's grey tomcat. This position lowered her under the horizon line of the hedge. Her companion, the trow Kellbrue, was of such a stunted height that, even standing as straight as he could, he was naturally hidden. However, Hugh barely even registered the presence of Kellbrue and the odd bundle that the trow carried. His eyes were on the selkie who blatantly wore her seal-skin wrapped around her slender, pearl-fleshed frame. Long black hair mingled wetly with the mottled seal-skin that concealed her immodesties. She looked up from the feline, and in her round face seal-black eyes found Hugh.

She knew him instantly. Without reserve she yelped, "Brother!" and sprang to him seeking an embrace. Hugh obliged, wrapping his arms around her. His chin propped comfortably atop the damp head that rested against his chest, sinuses filled with her salty scent.

Hulda watched from the corner of the rose hedge. Heartened by the warmth of the reunion, her attention drifted to the trow. His burden piqued her curiosity, so she asked, "Kellbrue, what is it that you carry there?"

He wrinkled his wide nose at her. "'Carry' would imply I'm moving, and I'll let ya know I'm quite pleased with standing still at the moment."

"What is it you hold, then?" Hulda countered. Though the trow could not lie it was sometimes difficult to get him to answer a question directly.

"Very little regard for the selkie wretch who made me come all this way," he snorted. By now the siblings had parted to watch as Hulda sighed and came down the road to lay a hand on Kellbrue's bundle.

"This, Kellbrue. What is this?"

The trow inclined his chin toward Hugh and answered, "Originally, his. 'Twas mine to safeguard, but fish-fangs over there has made a very good case for it to be returned. So, it is his again."

Hugh looked questioningly down at his sister, but her smug smile and narrowed eyes were determined to tell him nothing. So hand-in-hand they approached Kellbrue, and the fisherman released that touch when he reached out for the bundle. A quick shake unfolded it, revealing fins, body, tail and mask: it was a seal skin, and if it was his it had grown even while apart from him for it was full-size.

The selkie woman's smile became a toothy grin of excited joy as she watched her brother stroke the short fur of the hide.

"I know where Teran is being held," she revealed proudly. "And now you have a way to get there."

His moment of fascination was cut short by this reminder of the looming task ahead. Seeing the way his smile faltered, she reached out to gently touch his hand. Gazes meeting again, the selkie woman beamed. "Let me show you how it works," she invited, tugging him toward the sea.

"Coira!"

Hulda's sharp summons drew the selkie woman's attention to the spae-wife. An intense look was in Hulda's eyes when she asked, "How do you know where Teran is being held?"

"I've seen him. Not very close," she was quick to clarify, "because there are lots of old ones gathered around him. There are souls older than me there, and some may even be older than you, Hulda. I'd wager that the Huntress is, at the very least. And I was careful even with the distance: invisibility Seeming doesn't belong solely to the finmen, after all." Her wry tone slyly described one of the powers that was retained by the female finfolk who neglected to marry a mortal man.

Still, Hulda wasn't quite satisfied. "Teran's reach has grown unnoticed and is now apparently rather extensive," she warned. "Are you certain you weren't noticed?"

Coira tossed her head confidently. "Absolutely," she barked. Then, softening at the spae-wife's incredulous scowl, the selkie sighed. "Look, would you rather I teach him the unseeable trick first? Shapeshifting is similar to Seeming, anyway."

"That would be agreeable," Hulda allowed. "Every

time we do something near or in the water I believe Teran notices his presence. It is probably time to teach him to be hidden."

"I may as well be right now!" Hugh interrupted, waving the seal-skin in front of Hulda. "And if anyone cares to know, I also think this is a great idea."

Kellbrue brought his gnarled palms together in a pedantic round of applause. When he had three mildly annoyed faces looking toward him, he spread his hands plaintively. "This is all heartwarming and lovely and I'm sure it'd be a grand moment for some mediocre novel one day, but I have things to do. Ya know: corners to sweep, babes to swap in their swaddling wraps, cattle to mutilate, milk to spoil, or whatever it is mortals think trow do these days. I'm off schedule as it is, which I suppose is fitting, given how all the powers that be have gone cattywampus of late. Maybe I'll go rescue a kitten from some nettles; wouldn't that just be laughably out of character. Anyhow, am I being detained for anything else, seal-paws? The seal -skin is delivered, and so far as I know that fulfills my part here."

Coira stuck her tongue out at the trow. Withdrawing a leather pouch from the folds of her seal-skin, she dropped the purse into Kellbrue's waiting hands. It clinked merrily on impact, and he opened it while the selkie bid him off. "Our bargain is complete, Kellbrue. Away with you."

"That's fine silver," the trow muttered. He nodded approval and secured the pouch. "Lovely doing business as always, finling. Do me the kindness of leaving me out of the rest of this. Whichever way this turns out, I have a party to throw, either for the victory of another spin of the wheel or for the glory of the end of the world. Go team!" Plucking a reed from the roadside, Kellbrue shaped it with some mumbled syllables into a yellow-eyed, smoke-hide steed. The otherworldly horse allowed the trow to mount before leaping into the air. A distant echo of hooves on cobblestones followed it as the pair galloped after the tail of the dawn.

"What did you give him?" Hugh asked, curious what it would take to get a trow to part with a treasure. Admittedly, though, the seal-skin wasn't shiny and glamorous like the gold and silver pieces that had decorated Kellbrue's barrowhalls.

Coira shrugged, a gesture that seemed falsely lackadaisical. "Nothing much, just some silver coins."

"Where they your father's?" Hulda asked, and Coira glanced toward the sea almost fearfully. She quickly covered the reaction.

"Not yet," the selkie hedged. A finewife's duty was to engage with the mortals and bring silver to her finman husband, but in the lack of such nuptials anything Coira received was to go to her father. Negligence of this duty often earned a beating as punishment. To convince Kellbrue to return Hugh's seal-skin had taken quite a bit of silver, but Coira had known the danger when she'd made the offer. To her, restoring the skin to its rightful owner was more important than the threat of what her father might do if he found out about the trade. Besides, it was for the success of the Mither o' the Sea in the Vore Tullye. She hoped he would understand the necessity of the arrangement.

Recognizing that her answer was unsatisfactory for Hulda, Coira defended, "Regardless, he's sulked for too long that his plan for the changeling was spoiled. It's time for him to acknowledge his son, whose strength and victories will bring much renown to his name. So come, Hugh Reid, and follow a selkie to the sea. Shall I sing you the song we use on fishermen, if that is still all you are?"

She lifted her voice in a wordless melody, which was instantly familiar to Hugh's heart. Most recently he'd heard it on the evening that the sea had thrown his boat ashore, but his soul knew it from before then. It was a haunting, lilting, alluring song, and his feet wanted to follow it but his heart knew the truth of the being that sang it.

Hugh smirked at his sister, resisting the pull. "Shall I bring the dian-stane?" He asked Hulda, and the spae-wife shook her head.

"For this, it will do no good. It may only be moved from the table by your intent, so it is safe in my cottage. Go, learn your finfolk tricks, and master them quickly. Study them well, for they may prove to be key."

CHAPTER SEVENTEEN

It felt like the most natural thing to walk down to the seaside with his sister. When his mother died, Hugh's father had moved to Wales to be closer to his cousins. Fond of the archipelago and the lifestyle he'd grown accustomed to, Hugh had stayed behind on his parents' home of Rousay. Maybe he ought to think of them as foster parents, but he just couldn't frame that in his mind. They'd served the role. Since that separation, he'd fallen out of touch and into a complacent routine, but he hadn't felt a sense of truly being home like he did right now walking beside this magical, storied being that was amazingly his kin. Perhaps part of it was the exciting seal-skin in his hands. Perhaps part of it was the thrill of being on the edge of learning a secret that only a privileged few had access to. Perhaps it was a final acceptance of the truths the old stories were based on, which were at once more fantastic and more terrifying than they had been now that they were real.

Whatever the reason, a content smile warmed Hugh's weatherworn face as they maneuvered the pastures and fences. Observing the gallant creature beside him, who strode barefoot and brave among the thistle-grasses, who had defended him as though she knew him, Hugh wondered if she wasn't pleased that the planned marriage arranged for her had failed.

"What about you?" He voiced his question aloud. Looking into the seal-black eyes that focused on him, he clarified, "Did you sulk that our father's plan with the changeling failed?"

Coira shrugged. "For the life that was lost, yes, I mourned his death with the rest of them. But did I regret saving your life, which many say brought about the mortal's drowning? Not for a second, Hugh Reid. You are blood, and we should always take care of our own, regardless if they were exiled. And who says I want to marry a mortal, anyway?"

"Isn't that what mermaids are supposed to seek?"

"Oh, aye, if they want to be beautiful and pristine for the rest of their days. But with that comes a chain, for she is then linked to her husband's mortality and powerless to do anything about it. She trades her talents for pretty looks and a mundane mate who will die in the blink of eternity. She trades her fins for fidgets, and I won't have any of that. No chains for this selkie. I want to be wild," her voice cracked passionately, "and I want to keep enjoying my gifts, because that is better than shiny hair and perfect bodies. And anyway, wrinkles just tell the tale of all your laughter, and grey strands contain the wisdom of lessons learned. I welcome it!"

She ran into the frothing shallows and kicked a spray of water. "Hear me!" Coira roared to the sky, arms wide. "Bring on the hag in her own time! I welcome the crone, for in her is experience and power!" Whirling back to where Hugh stood on the shore, she barked a laugh.

"Still clothed, brother? Discard the human coverings and don your true flesh."

"What of the invisibility?" Hugh reminded Coira, though her raw enthusiasm was catching.

"The Seeming?" Coira rolled her eyes and heaved a sigh. "I suppose I did agree to teach you that first. Fine." She rolled her neck, popped some knuckles, and seemed to be stretching out to do battle. But then Coira spoiled it by widening her night-dark eyes and wiggling her fingers in what was surely meant to be a mystical fashion.

"Are you ready to learn the deepest secret of the mysterious finfolk, Hugh Reid?" Coira asked, and lost it with giggles before he could reply. "Well, too bad, because this isn't that secret. It's a good one, aye, but certainly not the deepest."

Grinning, Hugh found himself willing to try whatever Coira was about to recommend. Sensing his eagerness, she shrugged a little deeper into her skin.

"More than anything else, self-seemings are a matter of focus, especially the first few times. Have you ever meditated, Hugh Reid? No? Well, start doing that sometime. You know, after we're done with all this."

"But what if we fail?"

"Then you'll have a cold, bleak world in which to meditate, and honestly such an environment might make it easier to master. Now: invisibility. You don't actually disappear; that sort of thing is possible but it involves a lot of needless effort. Instead, the Finfolk way is to become unnoticed by the world, glossed over by the roving eye, because you have become so blandly one with your surroundings."

Thoughts wandering, Hugh recalled the way Hulda's cottage had looked like an unassuming pile of ruins at first, until Hulda had lifted that disguise from his eyes. She'd called that a Seeming then.

"Hugh Reid!" Coira barked, and clapped her hands together sharply. Startled out of his thoughts, Hugh was actually surprised to see that she was still there. And then it dawned on him.

"You were invisible just now, weren't you?" He asked, though he knew the answer immediately.

"Yes, but I was also talking, and it looks like you missed that part. Focus! If you know what to look for, and are actively looking for it, you can see through the Seeming. I had hoped you'd be listening intently enough to at least fight it a little, but I guess I'm just too good.

"As I was saying, the invisibility Seeming involves noticing everything around you without focusing directly on any particulars. Once you direct your awareness on a specific thing, you will be exposed again. You must acknowledge everything and nothing at once.

"Hear the movement of the ocean, and match to it your breathing. Breathe in as the tide comes in, and out as it leaves. Again, in with the water, and out with it too. In as it rises, out as it falls." She watched his chest move as, eyes closed, Hugh followed the instruction. After a few cycles Coira felt that his rhythm was even, so she added: "Feel the air as it moves against you, and imagine yourself as the breeze. It breaks upon you and you flow with it, eddying away until rejoined. Let it keep going where it will; you are one only when it touches you and during the short split after. Breathe in with the tide, and out; good.

Bask in the shoddy sunlight and shine with it, warming all the earth, the grass, the stones. Absorb all senses of the living world, be one with the energy around you. Breathe, and release."

Traditionally, water was the element involved with shapeshifting. As a finman, Hugh had a connection with the ocean on a primal basis. Coira knew all this, of course, which was why she started the meditation with the sea and kept a constant reminder on it throughout. That connection was the best chance they had for such an introduction, and Coira noticed that it was working when her gaze drifted naturally from Hugh to a flock of terns gathered on the shore.

"Good," she smiled. "Now do it with your eyes open. Let your vision slide over all, unfocused, like when you try to look in your peripheral vision without actually looking in it."

She could see that he struggled with that initially, but the invisibility effect was quickly restored. "Very good!" Cooed Coira. The time to really test him had arrived.

"There are some terns on the rocks. See how close you can get before they notice you. Breathe in, and out, and match your movements to the ocean's timing. Split the air as you pass through it, and swirl in the rejoining behind. Feel the grass crumple and give way underfoot, be the blade as it bends and lies flat. Breathe in, and out."

Since Hugh seemed to have caught on to the idea, Coira allowed her voice to fade with the last reminder. She remained in place so as not to spoil the experiment, and keenly watched Hugh. This direct focus let her see the moment he lost the game.

He made it quite close, to his credit. The birds remained at peace until one, probably a male, approached another with wings wide and neck lowered. The attacked croaked a loud, sudden challenge, and instead of letting the sound move through him Hugh startled at it and looked straight at the bird.

All of a sudden, the entire flock took notice of Hugh. A man stood inexplicably among them, which spooked dozens of sets of wings into rapid flight. Legs flailing and beaks agape with distress calls, the terns took off, wheeling as one to roost elsewhere.

They left Hugh in a shower of spent feathers and fecal debris; the result of birds panicked into flight. Lest he dislodge anything into his eyes, Hugh turned a slow circle in place. Following the sound of her shameless hearty laughter, he found Coira easily enough. No attempt was made to hide her amusement at his expense. Despite his embarrassment, Hugh couldn't help but smile right along with her. A chuckle even escaped him as he imagined the mess he must be.

As if to confirm that though, Coira bounded to his side and daintily plucked a feather from his forelock. "You are disgusting!" She declared, drawing the last word out with a throaty squeal. Grinning, she took his sealskin and shook it out to rid it of the discarded plumage.

"You know what the best way is to clean bird poop? A bath!" Coira thrust the seal-skin back into Hugh's hands. "You've got the basics of invisibility down, but you probably aren't up to maintaining it while playing in a new form. I'll keep us both hidden. You just enjoy. Now, because both of your skins already know this transition, all you have to do is focus to restore the connection. As you place the mask, feel its softness on your face, ears, the weight of the drape on the top of your head and in your neck. Let the body cascade down your back, and tuck your hands into the flippers. Envision how the back of your wrists feel to the pelt. Feel the webbing grow back between your fingers; the whiskers itch as they sprout from your, well, whiskers!"

She giggled, not just from the word play but also because the transformation was taking effect. Before her, the man stooped, shrugging into his new shape. It happened inside his clothes, so that as the seal emerged the human garments hung weirdly upon its curves. Coira solved the problem immediately. She hastily shucked the layers off before unwrapping and donning her own seal-skin. Coira dove forward, her metamorphosis taking place beautifully in midair, to land flippers-first on the rocky beach next to Hugh. Bristly muzzle nudged and snuffled the new seal, poking his limbs and bumping his shoulder with hers until he shook out of the trance.

His first attempt at moving failed. Accustomed to thinking like a two-legged being, his explorative steps as a four-legged land-awkward being were clumsy and uncoordinated. However, Coira was at his side. She shuffled forward a few feet to let him see how it was done, and by mimicking her motions Hugh got the method figured out. Within seconds they were down to the water's edge, and staring the surf in the eye.

It was actually a little daunting. Hugh hadn't seen the swelling sea from this lower perspective before, and it looked like the back of a massive beast the way it rose and fell as though with the act of breathing. There were dangers a-plenty in the ocean for a man in a boat, but there were far more for a fragile seal and those were just the natural ones. Add in the seemingly boundless threats of the supernatural and Hugh began to second guess whether this swim was such a good idea. However, Coira had no intention of allowing him to back out now. Determined that he should enjoy his seal form to its fullest abilities, she pushed and nipped until he bared his teeth at her. Even then she gently grabbed his forelimb with her mouth and tugged persistently. Finally, he sighed surrender and followed her into the water.

Swimming was a much more natural method of travel in this body than crawling. An effortless wave or kick powered him through the cold, salty depths as easily as an eagle soars. The rippling sea tickled as his momentum pushed his whiskers flat to his snout. When they surfaced for breath Hugh lifted his round head above the crests and was impressed by how far they'd gone in such little time. He turned, spying Coira's mottled crown to his side briefly before she winked and submerged. Ducking back underwater, Hugh watched her speed away toward a rock formation. She slowed, peeking back at him, and came toward him before reversing toward the rock again. Understanding the invitation to a game of chase, Hugh mentally shrugged. They were here and nothing had gone wrong yet. Why not? Working fins and body for the most thrust he could manage, Hugh darted after his sister seal. They improvised a game of tag in and around the stony stack and the volcano-dug channels. It didn't take Hugh long to master and enjoy how easily his blubbery body moved in the water. In fact, after a few minutes he realized that they hadn't surface to breathe, but his lungs weren't burning with need.

This surprised Hugh and his instincts almost boiled it into a panic until he understood that he wasn't drowning. Instead, he assessed himself and found that somehow he was indeed breathing; not as he was used to but rather how the Nuggle had described. Something about shapeshifting had triggered it, no doubt. Simply by being submerged, his skin had reacted and was peacefully coexisting with the sea, absorbing oxygen through that coexistence and passing it along just as his lungs would; just as a frog does. This wasn't anything to do with being a seal, Hugh knew, but everything to do with being a finman.

Thankful that it wasn't something else he had to actively think about, Hugh looked for Coira to re-engage in their game. Unknown to him, she'd used the moment of his introspection to sneak around behind Hugh. When he turned in his visual search she ambushed him from behind the rock formation. Momentarily taken aback, Hugh recovered quickly and pursued her fleeing form.

Looking back at him, Coira didn't see the massive black-and-white predator that loomed suddenly in her path.

CHAPTER EIGHTEEN

The impact of backing into something dense and alive was so unusual that it broke Coira's invisibility Seeming. Immediately, the orca sensed her presence. With an amazing agility that belied its bulk, it bent almost in half to bring its toothy maw into threat range of the seal. But she was gone just as quickly and the real chase began. Flaring and flapping madly, Coira's four fins and purpose-built body bore her rapidly toward the shore. The orca, keen on catching such an easy meal, pursued her fleeing form. However, Hugh noticed that it wasn't putting all of its effort into the hunt. Before he could think on it long, the reason was made clear.

A second orca moved in to intercept Coira. It asserted itself between the selkie and her goal, and when she flickered to the right the first orca was there to block her path. She scrambled left, and the second orca's mighty mouth gaped in a confident grin as it closed that route too. Having boxed their prey in between them, the two predators leisurely began to tighten the gap. Coira was left with just one chance, and as she twisted and turned to try to out-maneuver the hunters Hugh swallowed his fear and swam closer. Filled with trepidation but also with a fierce need to save his sister's life, he recalled the meditation that she'd taught him. Instead of allowing himself to fade from the world's attention, however, he projected the Seeming over Coira. Hugh envisioned the spots on her mottled hide to be just the rays of filtered sunlight, her body just a current combing through the tide, her energy just the ebb and flow of the ocean. And all of a sudden, with the abruptness of one jerking awake from a dream, the orcas deviated from their track. They drifted momentarily and Hugh could almost see their minds working as they tried to figure out how they'd lost their prey.

In their search they spotted Hugh, who in his urgent creation of the Seeming had neglected to include himself in it. He squeezed his eyes shut as their echolocating pops, whistles and squeals peppered him, filled his ears and body and lungs, just like the cold, cold water moved through him and with him. He was the dappled sunlight, the push and pull of the swell; he was the very salt within and without; and he rocked in the wake of the orcas, thinking only of the way that the water spun and whirled on the tail of their second failure. Giving up on this odd hunting ground, the whales carried on out to sea to find another one.

Hugh rode the meandering tide in to the shore, where Coira met him. She tackled him in the surf, chirping joyous sounds as she splashed a celebration. Hugh bared his teeth in a broad grin, marveling at what he'd just accomplished. They rolled together and their raucous barks stirred a nearby flock of sheep into a nervous patrol of their pasture.

Filled with a new confidence, Hugh wanted to share the story with Hulda. The journey back to her cottage would be arduous as a seal, and Coira hadn't told him how to shift back. However, Hugh's recent success inspired him to act on his own innate cleverness. Shouldn't it be the same as the technique used to become a seal, just in reverse? He decided to give it a try.

Closing his eyes, Hugh breathed deeply of the salt air and remembered what it was like to be human. To walk on two legs, arms long and swinging; to trace his tongue over flat teeth; the air cold and harsh against exposed flesh but playful in his hair. As he got down to individual fingers and toes and tried to wiggle and cross them, the transformation began. There was a fierce itching sensation under Hugh's chin. He moved to scratch it and the skin opened under his touch, enabling him to reach in and pull the hood of the sealskin off. The rest of it followed quickly, unwrapping from his pale human frame as though he'd only been wearing a one-piece jumper. He knelt naked in the rocky surf, shivering with the sudden exposure but also breathless from his victory.

Rather than throw it aside, Hugh absently wrapped the sealskin around his waist and midriff. He draped the mask and front flippers over his shoulder. A bone-deep weariness had come over him while kneeling at rest. Though he wanted to get up and go tell Hulda of his accomplishments, his will was held hostage by a body whose energy had been depleted. Hearing and smell became indistinct, and indeed the whole world seemed to fade away from him into a peaceful haze. Hugh's eyes closed partway under the heaviness of his fatigue, and his shoulders slumped in the surf. The tail of his sealskin washed back and forth with the waves.

The finman's fog expanded from his personal perception into the world around him. Coira, returning from retrieving the fisherman's clothes that now lay bundled in her arms, recognized the creeping tendrils for what they were. The fog enabled the fabled oarsmen to travel great distances in just a fraction of the time it would take a mortal. But where was he going? Coira dashed into the mist, determined to find out. At first she could not find Hugh, and she briefly panicked with the thought that she'd joined him too late. Her seeking intent twisted the path, however, placing her by his side. She took a knee next to him and perched her hand upon his shoulder; not hard, but firmly enough to be carried with him.

"Go on home, Hugh Reid," the selkie whispered to the finman. She focused her purpose on following his, and suddenly the fog had a new destination. It had tried to bring him to Hulda, but without a step in that direction it could not take him away from the sea. However, Coira's prompt of "home" gave Hugh's subconscious a new target.

The lapping sea remained the same, but the shale digging into their knees filtered away, becoming fine white sand. Both swayed a little as they settled in the new terrain. The muffled bleating of pasture-bound sheep was replaced by the strident shrieking of soaring seabirds. Slowly the fog faded away. It disintegrated in the sunlight to reveal basking seals and pearl-white buildings up the shoreline. Coira waited until she was certain of where they'd landed before she used her hitching hand to roughly shake Hugh's shoulder.

"Rise and shine, brother!" She trumpeted, grinning when his eyes opened and he straightened out of the trance.

Hugh blinked and peered blearily around. The moment of realization was obvious: he scrambled to his feet, spurred by the shock of their translocation.

"This can't - this is Hether Blether! Coira, what've you done?" Hugh exclaimed.

Rising with him, Coira lead Hugh by the hand out of the surf. "Wasn't me!" She replied smugly. "This was all you, Hugh Reid."

"COIRA, WHAT HAVE YOU DONE?!" Another voice demanded. Louder and furious like a blustering stormfront, the voice was also familiar. Hugh identified it even before he turned to behold the swarthy, dark-cloaked figure striding down the beach toward them.

"Wasn't me!" Coira repeated, though her voice had risen at least three defensive octaves. She side-stepped to hide partially behind Hugh, and the sorcerer mimicked her movement to keep her in his sights.

Pointing an accusing claw at Hugh, their father fumed, "There are many eyes on that man right now. We've worked hard to keep Hether Blether protected and hidden; hard work which you may have just single-handedly ruined!"

"I've got him hidden," she started to say, then fell silent as she recalled that the Seeming had fallen. Remembering that Hugh had saved them with his own, Coira checked but realized he had exchanged his illusion for shapeshifting and traveling. With a shrug, she followed up, "Well, I did. We'll just redo it."

"It is too late for that! You've come by sea and by magic, and every watcher will have alarms blaring." The sorcerer growled.

As if to prove his point, the flat, thick sound of air being bodily replaced popped in their ears. Hulda appeared in the source of it just a few yards down the beach. Crouched and clutching a cast iron stake, her star-stark clothing and plume-peppered hair whirled in the wake of her landing before settling gracefully upon her.

"Bah!" barked Coira's father, the sound one of seal-like aggression as he faced the intrusion of iron on his hallowed ground. "You see, whelp? This is what comes of meddling."

"'Twas you who meddled first, sorcerer," Hulda chided as she approached.

"For the good of a child!"

"Aye, and hers for the good of a world. My commendations to you both."

Coira's vindicated smirk sobered as the discourse continued.

The swarthy oarsman stamped his foot in the sand, and the power echo caused Hulda to stumble. She scowled as he spoke: "On with your portent that you may depart, witch! I assume you bring some raven-winged news to come here by way of iron."

Hulda confirmed his suspicion. Though his confrontational tone was disrespectful, so too was her conveyance of the stake. Allowing the latter as cancellation to the first, she explained, "Indeed, Finman, my message is grim. I have been given a vision concerning tonight's civil dusk. Teran has a dire force awaiting the thinning of the veil. He seeks to send not one miscreant, but many, to wreak what havoc they wish upon our world."

"Your world."

She ignored the poisonous correction. "This cannot be allowed. The time to strike is upon us. Teran must be contained and golden summer allowed to prevail so the Mither may heal the damage Teran's struggles have already done to the veil. If his monsters trespass tonight they will destroy what remains and shatter that which keeps the worlds separate. Even your people cannot dive deeply enough to hide from the Old Ones who thrive in the dark and the cold."

"And if the Mither regains control for her season? Think you Teran will be still come winter? The Vore Vellye will tear us apart regardless!"

"Think you the titans will help him again if he fails tonight? It shall not be. He has only come this far on their strength, and the titans will not back him a second time. Tonight we put the cycle back on its course, or let chaos reign."

"Let be what may be! Wherefore do you bring your doom-saying here?"

"The Warden of the Stone is here, and our means of reaching the place of Teran's struggles is here."

"Speak plainly, witch, if your need is so urgent!"

"We need the whales of Finfolkaheem! Gather your people to your winter sanctuary, and suffer us to follow. Your herd of whales dive deep and steady, and we must arrive by their carriage to maintain the Seeming, else we will never get close."

The sorcerer's features were somber and sullen as he weighed that request. Rather than immediately deny it, he seemed to be seriously considering Hulda's appeal. She was emboldened by this, and at risk of pushing too much she pressed him nonetheless.

"All we seek is passage," she assured him. "Bring your people below to safety and stay there. Spare just a few of your whales for our journey to the place of binding. And in this allowance, know you may well be responsible for our chance to save the world. Its fate is in your hands."

As anticipated, the additional push soured the Finman's expression. However, he turned to regard the crowd drawn by their interaction. It seemed as though all the Finfolk of Hether Blether had turned out as an audience and were now gathered behind him. Women, men, and children all watched expectantly in various forms: some seal, others humanoid, and divers presenting a form midway between the two.

Brusque though he might be, and ruthless in his dealings, when it came to leading his people the sorcerer always took their wishes into consideration. He assumed they had witnessed enough to understand the situation, and gestured with an open sweeping palm to Hugh, Hulda, and

Coira. "So? What say you?"

"Dive!" One swarthy man declared from within the shadowy mask of his sealskin.

"To Finfolkaheem!" A child squeaked from behind her mother's skirts, and giggled excitedly at the thought of the magical undersea world she'd only seen a few times yet.

As one the crowd murmured overwhelming consent, and the seals splashed and barked in the surf, bullying the waves in their readiness. Mermaids, who had watched while sunning on the rock-studded shoreline, slipped into the water in preparation for the inevitable decision.

Turning back to the three petitioners, the sorcerer shrugged. "Very well. For this cause you are welcome to Finfolkaheem. Come - we go to the deep and the dark, for only in the depths of the nightrealm does light truly shine."

CHAPTER NINETEEN

The island became a scene of bustling activity as the Finfolk prepared to leave Hether Blether. They put farming industries on hold, doled out some extra feed to lure their livestock into the stables should they need to retreat. Harvesting what was ready - the bounty of which surprised Hugh since the season for growth had barely even begun - they gathered once more on the shore. Coira's father silently observed their efforts until he was satisfied that all were ready.

In the meantime, Hulda turned to Hugh. "Your dian-stane is still resting on the floor beneath my table, Hugh Reid," she informed him, and smiled at his questioning scowl. "The cats knocked it off the table, as cats are wont to do."

"I thought you said nothing could move it except by my hand," he mused.

Hulda chuckled, though whether for fondness of her felines or for humor at his remark Hugh wasn't certain. "Normally, and with all else, this is true. However, I'm certain you've noticed that my cats are anything but normal." Her tone warmed proudly when she revealed, "I have heard of your successes in the ocean, and I know how exhausted you must be, but you must call the dian-stane to you 'ere we depart this place."

"Can't I do that at Finfolkaheem?" Hugh inquired, aware of the keenly disapproving stare coming from his father.

"It is possible, but the task will be simpler done here.

The dian-stane will find you wherever you can touch the ground, but it knows this place for here was it bound to you. The effort required and the toll taken will be less when done here."

He shrugged. "Very well."

"Kneel," she advised, "and place your palms to the sand." When Hugh eased into position she continued. "Reach out to your dian-stane with your heart and soul, and press into the earth. Will it to -"

"Oh!" Exclaimed Hugh as the sand suddenly condensed under his hands. His fingers gripped the smooth surface of the dian-stane and he straightened, pulling it from its salty berth. "That was easy," he marvelled at the eruption.

For her part, Hulda refrained from vocalizing the 'I told you so' that was foremost in her mind.

"Are we prepared?" The Finman demanded. With a proffered hand Coira helped Hugh back to his feet, squinting at the plain, round, hole-in-the-middle stone around which Hugh's other arm wrapped protectively. Hulda nodded.

"We are indeed, sorcerer," she confirmed, gesturing for the siblings to stand close.

"Very well. Stay within the bounds of the mist. Hulda, you must wrap your Warden in a Seeming to maintain the secrecy of Finfolkaheem. I charge you ne'er allow it to fade until you arrive to the binding-place. Hugh Reid, focus your thoughts on the palace of your birth. All

Finfolk are born at Finfolkaheem, and no matter how long you have been away the heart does not forget such a berth. But enough talk!" He raised his arms, and in that motion drew up a sudden fog from the land and water around them. The bank moved in with an astonishing speed, swirling 'round all those gathered on the shore. Hugh saw that the other finmen had lifted their hands as well, and with rotating wrists were maneuvering the tendrils so that the writhing mist was brought to heel.

"Let us be about it!" As one the group strode into the embrace of the lapping waves. Seals dove immediately below, fast on the sea-going mermaids' tails. The cloaks and draping garments of the swarthy finmen and crone-like finwives lifted and flared, revealing their true nature as multitudinous fins. As they waded in amongst the frothing currents the fins billowed and swept them powerfully into the sea.

Self-consciously, Hugh touched the rigid scar masses that lined his flesh where the finmen's fins began. He'd had the calloused growths since childhood, and now he knew why. His foster parents must have trimmed those fins and webbings, as any parent might do to such an obvious abnormality. Did they suspect it was a mutation, or did they ever wonder at the truth? What would they have looked like now? And was it too late - with all the magic he'd been exposed to recently, could it be possible to reclaim them?

Next to him, the seal he now recognized as Coira barked impatiently. They were the last two on the beach, and the fog line was beginning to thin. Even Hulda had gone ahead. Hurriedly Hugh shrugged into his seal skin, achieving the shapeshift. With the dian-stane held securely in his toothy maw he bounded head-first after Coira into the seething sea. The edge of the mist pulled in after them, leaving the hallowed island empty but for some small herds of bemused livestock tended by the marriage-bound mortal husbands the mermaids had secured.

The swim in the fog was one of the strangest things Hugh had ever experienced, and at this point that was fairly impressive. Though he felt the water move at the bidding of his flippers; though his whiskers were bent flush to his snout by the pressure of his traveling momentum; there were no visual cues by which to track his journey. Not even the dappled sunlight could penetrate the Finman's fog that magically truncated their trip. All was silence and muted grey mist, and the edgy sensation of frigid water getting colder without evoking even the slightest shiver in his blubbery seal form.

His relief at its thinning was swiftly overshadowed by his awe at what it revealed. More than once Hugh had found himself wishing that he'd paid more attention to Sigurd's stories, but even so he doubted they would have done Finfolkaheem justice. The massive coral-bound palace looked big enough to house an entire village or even a city - which, Hugh supposed, it must do. Its spiralling towers pierced miles high into the belly of the sea, almost disappearing into the inky black overhead. They were somewhere deep, that much Hugh could tell, but somehow there was no pressure bothering him. With a trust he hadn't had before but was now as strong as his former skepticism, he shrugged that concern away, attributing it to magic.

Bioluminescent seaweed thrived in acres of color and light that surrounded the palace in every direction. Their multi-layered tendrils waved hypnotically in the gentle current. The sight filled his eyes at first, until he was shaken out of it by a herd of gigantic whales that leisurely swam through his field of vision. Wide-eyed, his whole head turned to follow their flukes.

A throng of Eurasian otters rode in the whales' wake, nipping at their tails and harassing a calf so that it stayed close to its mother. Their efforts ceased at the two-toned howl of a hunting horn, to which the otters responded dog-like. The pack of them closed in on Hugh's father, pawing and circling and chortling a joyous welcome. Throughout the group, other finmen were greeted in a similar way by more rafts of otters that had swarmed from small kennel-like buildings around the grounds.

"They hunt with them," Hulda informed Hugh. Her voice escaped in a flurry of bubbles, and sounded oddly flat underwater. Still awe-struck, he was at a loss for words as the sorcerer circled back to them. Otters in tow, his stern features made Hugh wonder whether they were about to be chided for dallying. However, his words revealed quite the opposite intent.

"Come," the Finman invited. "We shall dine 'ere you embark. There is not time for rest, but we may at least prepare your strength for what is to come."

"A last meal?" Hulda inquired slyly.

The Finman looked directly at her. "Only if you fail." Their gazes met and held, and the water seemed to chill even further until Coira bumped Hugh's side. She swam forward, conveniently passing between the spae-wife and the sorcerer, and Hugh followed dutifully. The movement broke the contest on neutral ground. Not for the first time Hugh wondered at the animosity between the two.

However, his attention was soon overcome by the palace once again. As they approached its arched entryways, Hugh noticed that all Finfolk within it were in a humanoid form. Sure enough, once under the silver-etched eaves Coira sloughed off her seal skin to stride on two legs. Hugh copied her effort, though his transformation was less graceful as he juggled the dian-stane and secured his seal skin wrap with one hand.

Though Coira didn't laugh aloud at his awkwardness her eyes wrinkled and sparkled with mirth. She led him down the exquisite corridor; past courtyards filled with seaweed-draped statues of rearing pearlescent seahorses; past collection after impressive collection of silver souvenirs. Hugh's pressure-muffled hearing began to pick up the lilting song of a harp, its melody so complex that he guessed there must be several musicians playing together. However, the truth was revealed when they turned a corner and entered a cavernous room. In the corner stood a massive harp, and its myriad strings were attended by an octopus. The creature's lanky tentacles lay upon the instrument, sometimes using their tips to play and other times employing a quick pluck of a well-placed suction cup. Inexplicably, the soloist's wandering melodiousness filled the vast space, all the way up to the coral-encrusted ceiling which would have been obscured in shadow but for the flickering lights of thousands of radiant jellyfish.

Below, a low stone table supported an extravagant feast. Multi-colored cushions and pillows covered the floor around it, and upon these lounged many Finfolk. None had taken of the food yet. Rather, they seemed to be waiting for something. When Coira, Hugh and Hulda followed the sorcerer in, those already gathered remained seated but turned all attention to their approach. Once the four settled at their chosen places the Finfolk began to pass dishes and drinks around in a continuous flow of activity that didn't stop until each individual had plates in front of them piled high with a comprehensive assortment of seafood. Quiet conversations were contained at a private level and never compromised the lucidity of the lay.

Though Hugh did not recognize many of the arrangements, he nonetheless gave each morsel a fair attempt. Seated next to him, Coira helpfully identified the complexities - or, indeed, simplicities - of the individual dishes, but eventually Hugh began to tune her voice out. All of his attention was absorbed into his tastebuds, for each flavor was richer or rarer or brighter than the last. As far as potential last meals went, this was one for the legends.

Drinks accompanied the food, transported in stoneware kegs carved with dramatic images that featured great beasts and active scenes; Hugh recognized some - a broad-jawed leviathan on one, the infamous kraken on another - but most were well beyond his ken. A spigot near the base of the keg was released to dispense its contents into crystalline cups. The operation seemed to require a touch of finesse, as the pourer had to tuck the spigot under a corner of the seaweed mat which covered the cup, allocate the desired portion, then remove and close the spigot without allowing excessive interaction between the surrounding seawater and the draft. It was awkward at first, but Hugh quickly picked up the technique of moving aside the seaweed cover with his lips to drink. The mat was thick and shaped to the contour of its cup, and it immediately fell back into place.

Too soon, he eased back, settling comfortably on the floor cushion. Wrapped in the mental haze of a well-laid feast, he found himself longing for his stretchy lounging pants despite the fact that he was garbed in nothing but for the cloaking folds of his sealskin. Too soon, a wild tremor shook the seafloor and roused him from his stupor. The palace groaned, the platters rattled, and the musician carried on playing but with perhaps a questioning chord added to the harmonics. Too soon, a second quake followed, and under the expectant stares of the Finfolk Hulda stood. She offered a helping hand to Hugh, saying, "It is time we were about our purpose, Warden."

CHAPTER TWENTY

Hugh wanted nothing more than to stretch out on the floor cushions and sleep away the feast, the nightmares, the responsibilities, all of it. It would be so much easier than the task that loomed ahead of him. He'd been thrown full-tilt into a whirlwind of magic and myth, and the thought of rest was extremely enticing.

Hesitating, he allowed his gaze to wander, and naturally his eyes drifted around the room on a path as helter-skelter as those traced by the wee, iridescent shrimps that chased the feast's scattered crumbs. Many of the Finfolk seated at the table wore expressions ranging from anticipative to apprehensive, but his roving sight was arrested by the loving anxiety that wrinkled Coira's forehead. Her concern halted his subconscious search for some excuse to step aside. In fact, her very presence anchored him so abruptly that he reached out to tap the creases on her face in an attempt to clear them.

"It is easy to sit at the helm in fair weather," he murmured, quoting the Danish waterman's proverb.

"Where's the fun in that?" Coira rejoined, her teasing smirk easing back into place. It steeled Hugh's resolve, and with the strength of his sister behind him he swept his hand into Hulda's offered aid. Grip met grip and he gained his feet.

"Into the storm, then."

Coira's cool, smooth palm perched upon theirs to steady her as she stood. "You'll never know where to go without me. Remember, I've seen the place." She defied

Hugh's intercepting denial. "Into the storm!"

"The battlefield is no place for a selkie," the sorcerer butted in, stalling her enthusiasm. "I will guide them, Coira. No daughter of mine shall go to war if I am able; furthermore, this is not something normally asked of our chattel herd. In this, they will only obey a finman."

"There is a finman among us," Hulda pointed out with an identifying nod toward Hugh.

Smirking, the sorcerer condescended, "Maybe someday."

Hugh chose to recognize the pout on Coira's face rather than the implied insult from his father. He pulled his sister into a hug. "It's better this way," he assured her. "Watch for our return." There was so much more that he wanted to say, but it all sounded too final in his head. Rather than wish her farewell, he opted for a more optimistic parting: "We'll be back shortly, you'll see."

Coira eased back so that she could look him in the eye, and solemnly nodded. The sorcerer led the way out, but Hugh paused at the doorway and looked back. Though she stood and demurely watched them leave, he recognized the mischievous glimmer in his sister's seal-black gaze. She held a webbed finger to her lips to silently shush him, and promptly vanished.

"What are you grinning about?" Hulda inquired when Hugh caught up to them in the corridor.

"I'm just excited to finally be on our way," Hugh lied through his teeth. "Maybe I'll finally get some rest when we've won."

"You've been properly inducted into a world of legends and monsters, and all you are looking forward to is rest?" The spae-wife wasn't entirely convinced - Hugh could see it in the bemused half-smirk. But she shrugged and let him keep his secret.

They took a quick turn, cutting through a statuary garden and exited under a tall archway draped with seaweed tendrils. The dark green coils moved oddly in the current, and Hugh quickly noticed the cause: otter pups played amongst them, shepherded by a grey-muzzle female. They twisted and spun, cavorting within their little playground. The bravest spotted the trio and sailed down to circle them, drawing the others after him and rousing a series of irate calls from the elder otter. When the sorcerer waved them away she dove down among them, scattering the pups briefly. They came back together after a distance, swimming as fast as their wee bodies could go, and as they flew away like arrows Hugh's jaw slowly dropped. Along the sightline of their playful retreat, he was distracted once more by the meandering travel of the whale herd. The gigantic animals were closer this time than before, and about to be even closer: the sorcerer blew several blasts upon a curling shell, attracting the attention of the shepherds. Finmen astride draft horse-sized seahorses kept the herd together, and now, acting on the signaled command, changed its course.

The incredible experience of watching the mottled beasts swim directly for the trio was one that would be etched in Hugh's memory forever.

CHAPTER TWENTY-ONE

Down in the deep and the dark, the ice-cold ocean floor screamed and bucked. Tremors shivered this way and that as the bone and blood of the very planet was sundered, poured forth and clotted. Jotun - nine in all counting golden-haired Skadi - bent to the task of freeing Teran from his fetters. Two giants attended each limb which strained bound to the dusky rock by lava flows. Lightning leapt and streaked as Teran's attendants acted true to their infamy and blasted the bindings with stark hoar-frost; in the wake of the grinding meeting of molten and frigid the sparks sprang. Once the slightest shackle length ceased its pulsing glow mountain-born Skadi struck it with her hunting knife, breaking piece by piece from Teran's prison. The jagged light thrown by their efforts penetrated the depths like a mockery of the aurora far above.

In the glow of the lava, Skadi's pale flesh gleamed ivory-cream. "Soon you shall be free of this treachery, Njord!" She proclaimed, pausing to wipe the sweat from her brow. The core's inferno was too hot still for her to dare touch the foot of the entrapped god, but oh! she was close! In true irony it was she who was deceived, for to her eyes and ears the tortured, groaning victim was her estranged husband. Even whilst ensnared Teran was able to keep up the Seeming that beguiled her vision and made him appear to her not as the sneering, sunken-cheeked winter lord but rather in the fair-footed form of the Vanir god of the sea. Though she could not abide in his hall, nor he in hers, Skadi bore little resentment toward Njord in the wake of their divorce. Her sympathy was easily won by Teran's plea, and she brought with her the support of the frost Jotun that enjoyed her father's mountainous realm of Thrymheim.

The giants cared little for the discrepancy of identities between the god who lay before them and the one whom Skadi claimed they were there to rescue. Her fervor proved they were in the right place, and here they were presented with the mightiest challenge of prowess. They had been offered the chance to defy a titan at the behest of another, and the eight were pleased and honored to be chosen for such a test of strength. So they exerted their abilities to the very edge of their power, and slowly the Mither o' the Sea weakened in her renewing efforts; slowly the Earth's core cooled.

Absorbed so in her trial, Skadi ignored the small pod of whales that swam just outside of the lava's glow. She had something much more important to focus on than the biggest denizens of Njord's wretched realm. Already conned by a Seeming, it was almost too easy to hide the whales' cargo from her perception. The frost giants were trickier, but their focus too was upon the challenge presented to them. Once certain that the whales were benign they ignored the massive beasts, and it was simple magic to disguise the riders within the Jotun's unknowing complicity.

The three grasped long leads that wrapped around the bases of the whales' flippers - one on each - and came back behind the dorsal fin. There Hugh, Hulda and the sorcerer knelt or sat upon their respective mounts. In the lead, Hugh's father had guided them to the binding-place; behind him the spae-wife and the Warden rode abreast in a simple formation pattern. Hulda maintained the Seeming that allowed them to draw in close, and Hugh stared dumbly at the scene upon which they steadily intruded. It was nothing short of legendary, and once more the sheer weight of what they faced chilled him. What could he possibly do to help? Hulda and the sorcerer seemed so ready to simply do whatever must be done, but they were well-versed in this world of magic. To an undeniable degree, Hugh still felt like something of an outsider: a housekeeper with a brand new key to Edinburgh castle but no map. He had the tools needed and a vague idea of their use, but that was it. Now faced with the actual mess that needed cleaning, he wondered if they were in over their heads.

As if she sensed his sudden squirming doubt, Hulda glanced over at Hugh. Her fair features creased momentarily with concern for him, then eased as a smile gleamed from her. Indeed, its warmth seemed to caress his flesh, chasing away his worries and easing his fear. For that was what it was: fear of letting them down, fear of failure, fear so strong that it made him stop before he'd even started. But that wasn't right either. He'd started on this path, hadn't he, by riding a whale here; by returning a giant into its stone prison; by trading his body for a seal's. Maybe he could do this, and maybe not, but either way they were here and the moment was at hand. There was absolutely no turning back now, and while that finality had intimidated him before now his courage was up and he flashed a fierce, wild grin back at the spae-wife.

Skadi's blade skittered off a frozen section of lava and she vented her ire with a curse. She struck again, too wildly, and nicked Teran with the long-knife's tip. Her enchanted ears heard Njord's bellowing voice when he cried out, "Use caution, sweet Skadi! I'd like to live through this rescue."

"Aye, Njord, then hold still!" she chided. As though to herself, she added under her breath: "En kniv er ikke det beste verktøyet for å skjære is, men det vil fungere." The golden strands of her hair drifted like a gilded halo, and when a current carried a strand yet again into her eyes she snarled her Norwegian rant and threw her knife blade-first into the seafloor. Pale fingertips seized the delicate tendrils and wove them swiftly into knotted braids.

"There will be time later for that," objected Teran with Njord's scowl, and Skadi threw a frown right back at him.

"Easily said by the man lounging at his ease!" She countered. "What's your hurry, husband? No doubt you prefer the warmer embrace of these living chains."

"They boil the oceans, Skadi, wrought by the Orcadians' Mither o' the Sea. She's been driven mad by her perpetual struggler with Teran, and wants the whole realm for her own. The longer I am held by her the more these simple household gods will think they can oppose us! We must be swift!" His claims, coupled with the Seeming, were strong enough that Skadi heaved a sigh. Retrieving her knife, she assaulted with new vigor the lava sections frozen by her Jotun companions.

Their bantering continued as the sorcerer gently wheeled the pod back into the darkness of the deep sea. Once at a safe distance he brought the whales together.

"This doesn't look good," he commented blandly. Hugh couldn't help but nod in agreement.

Hulda, however, was pensieve. Faced with the foretold, she marvelled at how the Mither o' the Sea had already solved this for them even in the midst of her own battle. The spae-wife recalled the message that Hugh had brought back from his vision during the rest that had healed him from the Nuggle's death-bringing lightning strike. "The sea summoned the mountain and hides from her True Seeming," Hulda recited now. "Vengefully she guards him, seeing in his place another."

Hugh recognized the words; they'd been burning a hole in his soul ever since he'd heard them, still lingering even after he'd passed them on to Hulda. "You left out a bit," he spoke up, and was silenced by a scornful scowl from the spae-wife.

"I know I did," she countered. "It is irrelevant, at least in this moment. What matters is that we have the tools for our success before us; all we must do is seize them."

"And I thought the trow spoke in riddles," bemoaned the sorcerer. "All I see before us is a struggle about to be lost. Giants and old gods play against us. What is there available that may tip such weighted scales?"

Hulda smirked. It was a fox-clever expression that

dug wrinkles from her cheek to her nose to the twinkle in her eye, and Hugh knew it now. It meant that she had a secret, one that hid power within it. No doubt she was spinning some mysterious way in which to present it. However, they really didn't have time to waste on concocting the perfect reveal.

Voice deepening with an insistent fondness, he pressed the question. "Hulda, what is it?"

"The huntress," she obliged with an exasperated rush of a sigh. "The huntress!"

"Who, Ska-?" Immediately the other two hissed hushes at him.

"Not here, you fool! Say her name and she will take notice - and, so close, I do not want to discover whether or not she would look past your witch's Seeming!"

"Aye, not here, though not for lack of faith." Hulda rolled her eyes. "Neither speak the bound one's name," she added for Hugh's benefit. Judging by his annoyed scowl the impact of the lesson had hit home, and Hulda shrugged away the tension. "It is the huntress who will help us. She is a vindicator of balance, and once freed of the bound one's illusion she will be easily aligned with our purpose here."

"But what of the Jotun?"

Hulda clucked her tongue at the simplicity of Hugh's question. "Think, Warden! They are frost Jotun, and they navigate the lava with what might otherwise be named snowshoes. They are garbed in furs and hides - indeed, they attend to the huntress's blind goal! They are hers to command, no doubt come with her from her father's mountain realm. Turn the shepherd and the sheep follow! We must simply delay them until their assignment is changed."

Hugh and the sorcerer shared a grim whine as they contemplated Hulda's solution.

"So you will want someone to clear the huntress's eyes," the sorcerer extrapolated, "and someone to distract the Jotun. Mayhaps two for that duty," he mused darkly.

"What about Te - the bound one?" Hugh caught himself before saying the winter god's name, but maybe wasn't quick enough. He felt a dry cold trace over his shoulders and down his left arm until it reached the spot where he wore the dian-stane like a garter. Perhaps it was an irreverent use, but his forearm and elbow fit neatly through the central hole and it hung there comfortably, freeing both of his hands to grip the harness on his whale. It was convenient, and to be perfectly honest felt entirely natural, as if he'd always been meant to wear it there.

As though in response to his question, the massive creature that he rode emitted a low, crooning song; and in its four-way harmonics was a discernible voice. <WORRY NOT, WARDEN, SORCERER, SPAE-WIFE.> The Mither o' the Sea assured them through the whale-song. <I WILL MIND MY CHARGE. THERE IS SOME FIGHT IN SUMMER YET!> Her voice wavered in their minds, however, and she added, <BUT HASTEN NOW TO THE TASK AT HAND. RELEASE THE

HUNTRESS;

    BRING HER TO REASON.

    ONCE FREED MAKE YOUR CASE TO HER PLAIN AND SWIFT.

    HER MORAL HEART WILL RESTORE THE BALANCE.>

"Warden," Hulda beckoned, and Hugh reacted to the title, turning to look at her. "Do you recall what you learned with Yetnasteen?"

Sensing the purpose behind her question, Hugh swallowed his hesitations and admitted, "Aye."

"I bid you, by the huntress's step-daughter Freyja, goddess of war and of sooth-saying, lift the Seeming cast by the bound one. May the goddess guide you as she has before." In the wake of her fervent blessing Hugh was overcome by the sense of another presence nearby. It was the odd, shivery sensation one has when under scrutiny by someone else. Though he suspected the identity of the presence, his glance at Hulda's eyes solidified his notion. She watched him keenly, hungrily, unabashedly jealous of something no longer hers for the moment. He remembered something she'd told him once: she was merely a channel. For someone else to wield the power she was accustomed to invoked this reflexive response.

Noticing his curiosity, Hulda smirked; the expression had a little more tooth than usual, and seemed almost feral as she drifted between patrons. "Not to worry, Warden, a spae-wife is not bound to only one," she hissed lazily, eyes darkening even as he watched. "I have been around long enough to travel some. After all, networking is not just for businessmen." Hollow notes edged her normally warm voice, and the sorcerer drew upright as he realized whose presence now reared in the witch's shadow.

"Hecate," he muttered, not attempting to hide his awe. "We may just have a chance after all."

Not a scholar of Greek deities or a long-time worker of magic, Hugh was unfamiliar with the name. However, the reverent, almost cautious, way in which the sorcerer now beheld Hulda was enough definition for him; she had clearly secured another source of power, this one perhaps inclined to a more destructive end. The last was made obvious as she dropped the reins of her whale mount and, in a billowing flare-up of steam, summoned two spear-like torches. Holding one in each hand, she herself marvelled with the others at the defiant way in which the flames burned despite their watery location.

The arrival of these weapons also had the immediate effect of extinguishing her Seeming, which was made extremely evident by the ten pairs of eyes that suddenly keyed in on them.

"They seek to stop you!" shrieked Teran in Njord's voice. That was all the explanation that wrathful Skadi needed to hear.

"Fools!" she barked. In the echo of her voice pealed a distant wolf-like howl that chilled every ounce of warmth Hulda's smile had previously given Hugh. "Jotun, complete your task. I will disperse these miscreants."

"Warden, stay by me!" The Finman beckoned, and Hugh gladly urged his whale closer to the sorcerer's as the giantess began to move toward them. Though he wisely did not say it aloud, Hugh was reminded of Kellbrue's spiteful shout made in his silver-decorated barrow: "Protect your own, then, like a good Warden." He'd claimed the sorcerer and the dian-stane in that moment, and now it seemed his father was finally claiming him. The thought warmed him once more as the ocean between them and the huntress thickened, forming into a beguiling mist that Hugh recognized now. The fog enveloped the whole area, sweeping in from the darkness until it muddled all perception; and Hugh realized that Hulda had disappeared from their company without even disturbing her now-forsaken whale. A pained roar from the Jotuns' direction and a diffused white-orange bloom revealed her new location. The Finman had spun his fog and guided her through it so that she might launch a distraction. The rest was up to them.

Stinging cold knitted on Hugh's exposed flesh when the mist's droplets gripped at him as sudden frost. One shocked look at Skadi's approaching form, her hand outstretched claw-like and ice-crystal-clear, informed him of the source of the change.

"It is too late to hide!" Skadi scolded. "You have chosen to meddle in the affairs of bigger beings. Stand, now, and accept your fate!"

She clenched her fist and the mist shattered into billions of tiny frozen projectiles, and the Finman made an odd little cough: a quiet explosion of breath as he clutched at his heart. He wavered, and toppled as his mount and Hulda's abandoned whale wheeled to retreat. Instinctively Hugh reached out to him with the arm bearing the dian-stane, and steadily rotated his hand as though pulling the sorcerer in on a line. All of his intent was on hauling his father to safety. Miraculously, the sea obeyed: a willing current reared up to carry the wounded one to Hugh, who yanked him to his whale's back. His whale, that had remained calmly in service of the newly-claimed finman that rode upon it. Hugh mentally pocketed his giddiness for later, for Skadi had seen all.

"Most interesting," she acknowledged, curiosity narrowing her blue eyes.

CHAPTER TWENTY-TWO

Wrenching the dian-stane from around his arm, Hugh held it out between himself and the giantess. He didn't expect the chuckle that this move evoked.

"Child," purred Skadi as she prowled closer. "What do you hope to accomplish with a Faroe rock? Put it away and embrace your fate." Sheathing her knife, she unslung her bow and placed an arrow upon the string. Her motions were fluid, practiced, almost hypnotic in their easy confidence.

"Speak not of my fate when you don't even know yours," Hugh retorted impulsively. He focused on her through the dian-stane's center, wracking his creativity for the right words. What would lift the Seeming? He would have only one shot at this, he sensed. His thoughts implored Freyja for help.

Carried on the brunt of a searing comet, one of the frost Jotun flew between them. He hit the ground hard, shockwaves leaping out like spider webs in a radius from his impact. The white-hot flames sizzled out along those cracks, searing them shut with their incandescence. Within the embrace of the earth's new scars the giant twitched violently then lay still, and from the direction of his flight shrieks of taunting laughter crowed. Vengeful roars answered Hulda's victorious cackle, evoking a distant dialogue before pressure reverberations told of the continuing fight between the spae-wife and the Jotun. Unflinching in the passing heat, Skadi simply quirked an eyebrow at the downed giant. She sighed, shaking her golden head, no doubt pondering at the lack of good help these days. When she sighted again down the length of her drawn arrow at Hugh, she was surprised to notice a golden halo that wrapped his head and hands.

"What-" she started to ask, but the Warden seized the moment and interrupted her.

"Skadi, I beseech you, see truly! Look upon the bound one and see, he is not Njord. Feel the cold which creeps from him, hear the sliding glacier's scream in his voice."

To Hugh's credit, she glanced as he bid. Or perhaps not to Hugh's credit, for the words came to him unbidden. They sprang to his lips before he could conjure them, no doubt inspired by the goddess whose attention Hulda had blessed him with.

"Think, Skadi!" He continued, "What reason has this fate to befall upon Njord? None!" An idea abruptly came to Hugh, and he turned his intentions upon Teran. There - this was the way! He could feel the dian-stane ignite in his grip, and that heady rush of euphoria flooded his body, creeping with whiskey-warmth over every cell.

Hugh proclaimed, "This fate is not yours, Teran!" And when he did so, an odd pressure filled his skull, as though the entire universe had suddenly turned all its focus upon him. Still he steeled his resolve and continued: "You are part of a cycle, and it must turn. Nay, it will turn! This is the time of summer. Winter, remember your oath, and be bound!"

Noise flooded his ears as the two roared as one: Skadi in fury as the Seeming fell and she quickly realized the deceit, and Teran as his spell was disrupted and his scheme began to unravel.

Seeing the conflict now for what it truly was, Skadi threw her bow to the ground. She bodily shoved a Jotun out of her way to stand between them and Hulda, and began to cease the skirmish there. However, Hugh saw none of this. Taking advantage of the last chance he would have, Teran wrested an arm free of his bindings and flexed his claw-like fingers toward Hugh.

Even prone, his voice thundered with power. "Like the flower in frost, I command thee: wither!" Teran shrieked, and sundered Hugh's spirit from his body.

He drifted. Weightless, stress-free, directionless, peaceful. Somewhere in the corner of somebody's awareness - maybe his? - it reminded him of that half-sleep state: not waking, not sleeping, when you might hear the voice of a lost loved one. He was an echo, a twitch away from sleep paralysis when the mind jump-starts the body with the spasm that saves you from falling. He was a ghost, with neither impetus nor power for the earth-shatteringly loud scream that might - just might - register in the waking world as a whimper's whisper. Cotton-soft silence filled him, cushioning his awareness and surrounding him with the grey half-light of pillowy, carefree nothingness.

Hugh's body slipped from the back of the whale, a languid arm falling heavily across the Finman's frame and pulling it down too. With no rider to convince it otherwise, the whale kicked its mighty flukes and gave chase after the others' retreats. Its whirling wake tousled the two bodies and delivered them softly to the seafloor.

In seconds Hulda was there beside them. She lay the torches upon the ground and the eight Jotun maintained a respectful distance of the sputtering steam geysers they cast. Skadi stepped closer to investigate the Warden and the sorcerer.

"Neither is dead," she announced, while Teran cackled lowly even as the lava bindings closed fully upon him. With no more challenge to her waning strength, the Mither o' the Sea was finally able to wrap the molten coils tight and secure her adversary for her summertime reign.

"The sorcerer has no pulse," Hulda protested, moving from him to Hugh.

"Certainly not, for his heart and his workings are locked in hoarfrost. Regrettably," Skadi admitted, "the fault is mine. However, this is a boon disguised, for he is thus mine to restore. Behold!" She laid her hand upon the Finman's chest briefly, scowl thoughtful as she reversed her earlier workings, and after a moment the sorcerer's limbs thrashed in a promising way and his swarthy complexion flooded his flesh once more.

"What of your Warden?" Skadi inquired, noticing the pensieve expression on Hulda's features.

Hesitating, the spae-wife picked her words carefully. Though the huntress was helpful now, it was hard to predict how that might change if she (or her attendants) sensed weakness. Slowly she answered, "His body is well; nothing is wrong that I can tell. But his soul is...elsewhere.

I can feel its thread, and it is tensioned, but its end is not within my Sight."

Skadi grunted. "You, young one, need a valkyrie. My duty here is done, my trespasses all reconciled. Blessed be." The waters froze under her snowshoes, providing solid steps as she and her Jotun companions departed the scene. Left alone, Hulda contemplated her suggestion.

"A valkyrie, or a chooser of the slain," she mused, and reached out with her mind, her faith, and all her energy once more. "Freyja, I implore you, find the Warden of the Stone, Hugh Reid, and return him to the living shell he has left. He may not yet be in your realm, but lost on the roads in between. Be swift as raven-flight for if this separation goes on too long I fear he may wander forever." Hulda sent her prayers forth with powerful intention, and planned her explanation for when the sorcerer awoke.

Time had no business here. Hugh had no reason to wonder how long he'd drifted despondently. He had no thoughts, truly, nothing so intentional as that. So when the mockery of a raven coasted by, its form indistinct yet undeniable, it passed barely remarkable. It was merely a brief blot in the murky effervescence; its croaking call reverberated faintly in the muffling grey. And then it too was gone.

"We should move him," the sorcerer suggested, his voice hoarse from the trauma inflicted upon him.

"No," Hulda insisted. "She will find him. Moving him may make it more difficult for him to find his way back."

<HUGH REID.>

The voice was familiar in a vague fashion. Moreso than its sound he recognised the way it existed only in the space between his ears. And since he was only a reflection of that body, it seemed to surround him.

<HUGH REID.>

Perhaps it was most heavily focused to the right. His awareness turned that way, slightly, like a newborn babe's face is drawn to the direction from which his suckling body's warmth comes.

<SEE ME, HUGH REID. HEAR ME AND KNOW ME. YOU WANDER, AND I HAVE BEEN SENT TO BRING YOU BACK.>

See? But how? Perhaps, if he focused on that voice, and opened his awareness as if opening his eyes, he might see. He imagined drawing in a breath, but through him, as with a Seeming of invisibility, and was rewarded with a blinding, almost painfully bright wash of light. Before he reflexively shut that semblance of seeing, he identified the kelp-draped horse-like being that was by his boundless side.

<OH, HELLO.> He replied to the Nuggle.

<GREETINGS, HUGH REID.> Yes, there was that smugly amused tone. He'd missed it, Hugh realized.

<AREN'T YOU DEAD THOUGH?>

<AYE, SUCH EVENTS DID TRANSPIRE.>

<SO IF I'M SEEING YOU AND TALKING WITH

YOU, I MUST BE DEAD TOO.> It made sense, in the oddly but comfortably detached way that everything here made sense.

<INTERESTINGLY, THAT IS NOT YET TRUE. THIS PLACE IS BETWEEN PLACES. YOU ARE NEITHER DEAD NOR ARE YOU ALIVE. THIS IS A PLACE NOT UNLIKE THE FINMAN'S MIST.>

<I'M A-DRIFT.>

<AYE, THE WORD IS SUITABLE. TARRY HERE TOO LONG AND HERE YOU WILL REMAIN. ALREADY YOUR FATE-LINE DIMS.>

<MY...WHAT?>

He sensed the Nuggle's psychic shrug. <IT IS SOMETHING THE GODDESS FREYJA REQUESTED THAT I SAY. SHE SENT ME TO FIND YOU AND TO GUIDE YOU BACK. SHE SEEMED TO THINK YOU WOULD UNDERSTAND, BUT I SUPPOSE IT DOESN'T MATTER. IT IS MERELY A WARNING OF THE NEED FOR HASTE.>

Haste, always haste. Why couldn't he enjoy a moment of rest? Whenever he managed to get a whiff of peace something seemed destined to rush up and tear it away.

"Hugh Reid!"

The recognition of that voice shivered through him like a jolt of electricity. He ripped that sight awareness open once more, squinting in the brilliant glare. And there she was: Coira, leaning over him with her dark hair damply framing her pale face. There were two others with her; their features slowly came into focus, but the effort became too much for him and his sight awareness collapsed, shutting him back down into the fog.

"No! We had him!" Moaned Hulda.

"Do it again, girl," the sorcerer bade Coira. Initially when she had dropped her Seeming and revealed her stowaway presence, her father had been furious that she'd disobeyed him. However, when she insisted that she could help, he was forced to acknowledge that her unique magic may be of applicable use.

Coira was already humming when he barked that order. It was the siren song, the beguiling magic of selkies and mermaids. No fisherman could resist its lure, and though Hugh began his life as a finman he'd spent is as a fisherman. She used her song now to lead this one not to his entrapment or death but rather to life.

<FOCUS ON HER VOICE,> the Nuggle advised him, <AND FOLLOW IT LIKE YOU DIRECT THE MISTS TO SHORTEN YOUR TRAVEL.>

<I'VE NEVER DONE THAT THOUGH,> argued Hugh.

<YOU HAVE! THAT IS HOW YOU CAME TO HETHER BLETHER THE SECOND TIME. YOUR HEART AND SPIRIT KNOW THE WAY. ANCHOR ON HER VOICE AND PULL YOUR SPIRIT HOME.>

Turning his focus as the Nuggle suggested he pushed his awareness toward Coira's voice. When that didn't seem to do anything Hugh altered his tactic. He envisioned the her song as being behind him, and allowed himself to be pulled backward toward it.

<FAREWELL, HUGH REID.> The Nuggle's voice whispered distantly as Hugh's soul was reeled in down its fate-line.

CHAPTER TWENTY-THREE

"I just want to go home," Hugh muttered, to the surprise of everyone gathered around his bed. As soon as he'd awoken on the sea floor, the sorcerer whisked them away to Hether Blether. Technically it was closer than Finfolkaheem, and since the majority of his people were tucked away in the safety of the underwater kingdom it was a more tactically sound decision. Their struggle seemed to be at a rest, but the sorcerer preferred to err on the side of caution. Hether Blether's location was already compromised; if anything were to follow them, let it follow them there.

The invisible isle was also an easier place for Hugh to recover, since he did not have to maintain the thin-skinned exchange that allowed him to breathe underwater. He lay prone beneath the sheepswool blanket, just breathing. Everything hurt: his body, his heart, his soul. He was so overwhelmingly tired that all he wanted - no, all he needed - was some time alone in his quiet, familiar house.

So, when the sorcerer gruffly offered Hugh a place to live at Finfolkaheem and Hether Blether, he declined. When Hulda volunteered to ready her guest room for his residence, he declined. And when Coira, initially offended and confused, demanded to know why, it took Hugh a moment to put his feelings into words.

"I've lived most of my adult life alone," he finally explained. "That's what I'm used to. I'm comfortable that way."

"You'd have your own space here," Coira pleaded,

but Hulda, with her cheshire smirk, shook her head.

"It's not the same," she commiserated with Hugh, as one who also lived without the company of other people. She couldn't say she lived alone, however. And now, having been exposed to the arcane, Hugh would never live alone again either. That was his realization to make, however. Sympathetic of the lessons he still had to learn, she consoled Coira instead of continuing to pressure Hugh.

After a day or so of recuperating on the fabled island, Hulda deemed Hugh fit enough to return to his home on Rousay. The sorcerer obliged him a boat ride and Coira accompanied his swim to the shore. There Hulda waited, garbed in billowing white and gold as before, with her grey Jaguar purring on the side of the road. They rode through the rain in silence, with Hulda watching the bumps and potholes ahead while Hugh supervised the passing of the countryside.

They passed the occasional old crofter out tending a field or a flock, but everyone on Rousay knew Hulda's vehicle. None who observed them waved, though most inclined a chin or lifted a hand in a gesture of respect; or perhaps of warding. As a spae-wife her knowledge of healing and of the natural ways was crucial on the island, but the old superstitions were ingrained in the people of the land. Awe was always close on the border of fear.

It wasn't long before they came upon his driveway. Hulda turned the car onto the gravel, and touched Hugh's elbow as he stirred to exit. "You are welcome to call anytime, Hugh Reid," she assured him. "It goes without saying, but thank you. There are none who would have done what you have done. Take what time you need, but know this: the world is better with you in it, not just on it."

He met her gaze, tempted to ask what she meant, but nodded and turned away instead. He had a pretty good guess. Gathering his dian-stane and his sealskin he mounted the stoop. A note stuck to the door caught his eye, not least of all because its thorn-nail also held aloft his mother's necklace, once stolen by Kellbrue. The message was simple: "You're out of milk and honey. Cheers, Kellbrue."

Opening the unlocked door, the first thing Hugh noticed was that somebody - no doubt the trespassing trow - had cleaned and organized every room. He'd raided the milk and honey, no doubt as payment like the stories told, but all else was tidy and neat. The new addition of a small chair made of woven reeds perched at his hearth warned Hugh that the visit would be repeated.

Hugh unloaded his burdens on the kitchen counter and meandered back into the living room. There he eased into his recliner, relaxing muscle by muscle gradually until every ounce of his weight was surrendered to the chair. He puffed out a sigh, emptying his lungs and his body of tension, and closed his eyes.

The clock in the bedroom ticked the minutes away, and the ever-present wind whistled through the neglected stones in the garden, but inside the house all else was silent. He absorbed that silence until the muffled sound of old electrical wiring within the walls seemed as loud as a scream between his ears. Then, he pulled his feet beneath him once more, and checked the day of the week on his weather station's display. The device was critical to his work as a fisherman, and now to his sanity. He felt as though he'd been disconnected from the mundane world, transported to a place not as concerned with caging time in a daily measurement. Now it helped him return to the organized human world, if just to acknowledge by the weekday that the Taversoe pub was currently serving patrons. And that meant that old man Sigurd would be there. Hugh had some pride to swallow.

He went out front and was reasonably surprised to see that his trusck was missing. It took a moment to remember that he'd taken it to Muckle Water back when all of this had started.

"Not the first time I've walked to and from the pub," Hugh reminded himself and set out on foot. The thought of shortening the distance with the Finman's fog crossed his mind but he pushed it aside almost immediately. He needed a break from all of that. He needed a little normalcy again. Besides, it was only three miles or so.

His brisk, long-legged stride delivered him to the Taversoe in about an hour, and he spied a familiar pair of shoulders hunkered at the bar. Crossing the cozy dining area to the half-dozen row of stools, Hugh settled astride one of the cushions beside Sigurd.

Getting the attention of the bartender was easy, and when Hugh stated that he would be paying Sigurd's tab for the next month, starting today, getting the old man's attention was even easier.

"To what do I owe the favor?" Sigurd asked, his craggy features furrowed with bemusement. "A man can put away a fortune of free whiskey in a month's time."

"Maybe a man should drink at home sometimes," Hugh replied, smirking in the warmth of the hollow threat.

"Now, you know what the missus thinks of that sort o' thing."

"Aye, she matches you cup for cup, which is why you come here, so your bottle at home doesn't empty quite as quickly."

"You've got me there, lad," admitted Sigurd with a chuckle. "Let's have a dram of Orkney's finest for my benefactor, will ye?" He requested of the bartender, who obliged him swiftly. Passing the highball to Hugh, Sigured queried again, "Come now, lad, what's inspired the open wallet?"

It had been...Hugh wasn't certain...days, maybe weeks since his last sip of scotch. He savored the burn which started sweet on the tongue and spread all-encompassing down his throat and into his chest. Only when the tingle came back to his cheeks did he respond: "You were right."

"Oh, is that so? What about?"

"Everything," Hugh answered vaguely, another sip poised at his lips. Sigurd waited expectantly until the whiskey loosened Hugh's words enough to elaborate. "The stories, you know. Trows, nuggles, finmen, selkies, all of it! You were right."

Closing one eye as though to focus on him better, Sigurd scratched the edges of his white beard and shrugged more comfortably into the embrace of his grey knit sweater. "You were always a skeptic, Hugh Reid. Why the change of heart? Surely you must think they're still naught but stories for the very old or very young."

"No, I was wrong, and what's more, I've seen them." He whispered quickly when the bartender went to check on a visiting couple who were lodging in one of the Taversoe's rooms. They occupied a table at the far side of the dining area, taking advantage of the large picture window that looked out upon the nearby loch. As the bartender walked over to inquire about refilling their glasses, Hugh urgently revealed to Sigurd: "All of it's real. I...it's so hard to describe. I helped with the Vore Tullye, Sigurd! I lifted a Seeming from -"

He stopped when Sigurd cut him off with a raised hand. There was a cautious tension in the old man's winking eye. "You're starting to sound like that spae-wife Hulda, Hugh Reid. I don't know what a fisherman's doing getting involved in all that, and frankly I don't need to know. I'm just a simple old storyteller. But maybe I've heard a new tale just recently, about a man who discovered a power hidden within himself. He learned how to wield it in amazing ways and accomplished legendary feats, even saved the world from a fate of endless winter. Maybe he found a new part of himself that had been lost, or maybe he knew himself all along and needed a little nudge to realize his full potential."

"Or maybe he was happy just as he was," Hugh objected, understanding that somehow Sigurd already knew of the events as they had transpired. How? That was the real question.

"Maybe," Sigurd allowed with a smirk. "But I doubt it, just as I doubt this is the end of his story. A man's true purpose, his true self, the immortal childlike wonder that pushes him to get up and do something; this has a way of resisting stasis. One cannot look out his window all his life at the mountain peak and merely remain curious as to what is at the top, or what the view of his house is like from the summit. Eventually, he will make the climb. The moment of calling will present itself and if he is ready he will answer it. If he is not ready, then it is not truly a moment of calling. The soul has a way of knowing its purpose."

Slowly, Hugh asked, "Do you mean this was all fated to happen?"

"What do you think?" Sigurd countered. Finishing his scotch, he gathered his long-tailed coat and his hornbeam walking stick. "Like a compass will always find true north, the soul will always find its purpose. Try denying it, turn it about, and eventually it will come back around to its course. If you have doubts, give it a try. Thanks for the drink," he touched his forehead in a farewell salute and left Hugh deep in thought at the bar.

CHAPTER TWENTY-FOUR

The Warden of the Stone decided to test Sigurd's theory by being a fisherman again. He retrieved his truck from its roost at Muckle Water, hitched up his boat trailer, and for a few days he did his best to avoid anything supernatural. The first day came and went without remark, which gave him some hope. When the sun rose on the second day, Hugh awoke somewhat confused as to where he was, but he quickly remembered and went about his attempt at mundanity. However, on day three he found himself wondering whether he could use the finman navigation talents and his own connection to the world rhythm to wrap target fish in a custom current and pull them to his net.

That was the moment when he realized that maybe this wouldn't work.

So he tried to live a balance.He manipulated the sea and its denizens to his favor, earning more in that week of fishing than he had in the whole month prior. Hugh kept a ready supply of honey and milk available because that was more convenient than cleaning his house himself. Kellbrue or another Trow visited at night periodically, which resulted in a depletion of his milk and honey but also in cleaned and sorted dishes, dusted surfaces, and shined glass.

Everything else, though, Hugh did without magic. He cooked his meals, if only because he hadn't learned how to manipulate that task. He walked to and from the pub, except for that one night when he wanted to get back home faster and travelled within the Finman's fog. And finally, when he admitted to himselfg that this new lifestyle was more interesting and easier in some ways, he dropped hisi last lingering inhibitions.

Weeks later, a perfectly natural rainstorm raised the waterline of Muckle Water, and as he towed his trailer by the loch Hugh couldn't help but think of the Nuggle. Was it still wandering in limbo? Or, rescue mission complete, had it crossed back over to whatever restful realm from which Freyja had summoned it? That evening, when the brilliance of the midnight aurora woke him from his whiskey-induced stupor, Hugh decided to find out.

He'd been ruminating over the disemboided state into which Teran had sent him. Was there a way to do that from his own intent? Now, watching the way the sheets of colorful vwapor danced and flickered over the steam from his tea, Hugh imagined that they resembled a curtain. Was it too fanciful to suggest that on the other side of that curtain lay the spirit world? There was probably a story somewhere that gave it such a role. He remembered - too well - how it felt when his soul and body were sundered and left connected only by what the Nuggle had called his fate-line. He remembered with every sober dream how traveling down that line and back into wholeness had felt. There was a reason he drank himself into unconsciousness every night since.

Well, his cabinet of sleep remedies was at a critical need of restocking, so he probably could expect to be awake for the rest of the evening. Why waste it? Perhaps he could cushion the journey with the Finman's fog.

Hugh finished off his tea and set the emptied mug down to nest amidst his garden's cracked pavers. Stepping out to what seemed to be the most appropriate place, he knelt in the shallow circle left bare by the removal of the dian-stane that had rested here for so many years. Now it waited under his bed, for the idea Hugh had in mind did not require its assistance.

Kneeling in that circular hollow, he pressed his denim-clad knees into the cold, soft earth. The sapping chill permeated the heavy cloth, giving his flesh the impression of dampness that was absent and yet always present on these northern islands. He held that reassuring coldness in his mind, fixing it as his grounding place, the place in which his body would remain.

Now for the tricky bit. Hugh spread his palms across his thighs and took a moment to mentally scan his body. Once confident that his frame wouldn't just collapse and fall over, he took in a deep breath and sent his gaze skyward. He let the soaring lights of the aurora fill his vision. It filled his sight, his being, everything that made up his mental clarity, and just when it seemed that he might burn up in its splendor Hugh summoned the Finman's fog into his focus and hurled it into the gale with all the intent and psychic force that he could muster. He imagined it draping over the flashes and folds, and in its wake he exhaled and cast his soul.

His body sagged and eased onto its side as the energetic will supporting it rocketed into the aether.

CHAPTER TWENTY-FIVE

Though his initial intent was to find the Nuggle, his cast-off into the realm between realms quickly became a scramble for control. Like a man overboard surrendered to the tumultuous sea Hugh fought for some sense of direction; of up, down, or any hint of how to see anything besides the grey eddying mist.

Finally, he realized that his hasty flurry of panic was the very thing keeping his head metaphorically underwater. With a renewed focus on the Nuggle - how it smelled, how the slick seaweed mane was cold under his hand, how its pyschic voice was everywhere and nowhere all at once - he set the waterhorse as his anchor and pulled his spirit down the line. And it worked!

Like a boat with a newly seized rudder, he swayed under an abrupt change of course. The mist thinned to a tunnel; he could see fairly well ahead of him but the edges maintained a healthy haze. Casting about to get his bearings was complicated, as Hugh had never seen Rousay from above before. However, the familiar mossy grey Yetnasteen caught his mind's eye, and he drifted down closer to the Giant Stone. From there, he focused again on the Nuggle, and realized his anchor-line stretched toward Muckle Water. "How appropriate," he mused.

In a blink of motion his astral awareness transported to the humble loch where the Nuggle had died in a lightning strike meant for Hugh's own demise. He thought at first that he'd been mistaken, for the loch seemed empty of life. Then, a ripple broke the mirror-calm surface. From its center reared the kelp-draped head that Hugh had hoped to see. Dark eyes fixed on him, and in that solemn horse-like face the Warden glimpsed a very human hint of pride.

<WELL, WELL, IT SEEMS CONGRATULATIONS ARE IN ORDER, HUGH REID.>

He grinned, pleased by the recognition of his achievement. Excitement mounted as the pale head moved closer and the Nuggle rose from the loch. The great beast that had diverted from its game of luring mortals to their watery deaths in order to teach him so much stopped just in front of him in the shallows. There it knelt as before, and this time Hugh stepped to its side with none of his previous hesitation. He slid a leg over the damp back and settled astride the Nuggle as it stood once more.

<WHAT DO YOU SAY WE GO FOR A RIDE?> The Nuggle suggested, and Hugh, who now felt more at ease looking at the backs of those pointed ears than at his truck's tattered steering wheel, admitted, "I'd like that."

Expecting the waterhorse to turn and plow through the loch, he was caught unprepared for the lurch as the Nuggle gathered itself then leapt into the air. Hugh yelped aloud, clutching at the seaweed strands as the Nuggle's legs and neck pumped in its efforts to climb skyward. The motion was not terribly different from its swimming movements, only unanticipated.

Quite forgetting that he himself had been airborne moments prior, Hugh exclaimed, "You're flying!"

<INDEED,> the Nuggle confirmed with a mental

chuckle. <WE ARE BUT SHADOWS HERE, NO LONGER BOUND TO THE GROUND. WHY NOT FLY?>

"Why not," Hugh agreed, caught up in the exhilaration of the wind against his face and the world far below. He clenched the Nuggle's mane in sudden fists, impulsively shrieking "WHY NOT!" once more to the heavens. Oh, to watch the landscape spin beneath! Oh, to be liberated - Hugh roared aloud his wordless exuberance, and the Nuggle joined in with a mighty whinny as they chased the boundless horizon.

The clarion call of a hunting horn made the Nuggle pull his charge up short. A second blast answered the first, evoking a shiver in the waterhorse. It rang so near to Skadi's wolf-howls that Hugh nearly dove for cover before he recalled that the mountain-borne goddess was now on their side.

"What is it?" Hugh asked, searching the edges of the mist for clues.

<BE ON YOUR GUARD, HUGH REID. PERHAPS FLYING WAS NOT THE BEST IDEA,> advised the Nuggle as it descended slowly, then faster when a third horn sounded. By the time its hooves touched the earth a fourth reply was made, and suddenly the air exploded with activity.

Riders of all sorts came charging from the hazy boundary. There were so many that at first it seemed they surged from all directions, but it quickly became apparent that the raucous host followed a leader's path. The swirling line of huntsmen trailed the spectral, eight-legged horse whose mighty hooves pawed the air at the bidding of only one being.

"Oh no," Hugh whispered, realizing what the Nuggle had already surmised. "This is the Wild Hunt."

<INDEED,> confirmed the Nuggle darkly. When encountered by a mortal in the waking world, the Wild Hunt was often an omen of death or other impending misfortune. But what could it mean for Hugh to come across it here in the spirit realm?

The leader of the Hunt drew up short directly in front of Hugh and the Nuggle. His followers fanned out behind him, finally slowing enough for Hugh to count their number. Twenty-seven were the huntsmen, some of them translucent and sunken-cheeked like ghosts, others radiant with high-reaching points on their ears, and all in between presented a myriad arrangement of legendary humanoids. They flew astride red-eyed horses black as pitch and jet-furred stags whose grasping antlers twisted crooked as crabapple boughs. Between the many hovering hooves wove the dogs: like hellhounds straight from a cultist's worst conjuring they prowled in and out of the shadows, and so in and out of perception. Their toothy, parted jaws drooled sulfurous smoke, and their eyes stared saucer-like and unblinking. For his part Hugh met the gaze of one for a brief second, then looked quickly away for fear that he may never breathe again.

His scattered survey settled on Odin, the leader of the Hunt. Shaded by his wide-brimmed hat his single eye sparkled with what emotion Hugh could only guess. Two massive wolf-like shadows guarded Sleipnir's flanks, eight hooves and eight paws standing maddeningly flat upon the air some three feeet above the ground. Perhaps the ground itself wasn't even there at all, though, and the Nuggle only appeared to stand upon it simply for the sake of Hugh's sanity. They were, after all, theoretically incorporeal -

"HUGH REID," boomed Odin, shaking the Warden right out of his reverie.

Quite unaccustomed yet to addressing gods, Hugh managed an awe-struck, "Er, good day, Odin."

"And so it is, Warden, so it is. You have achieved something great, and with so little time to prepare. Balance is restored to the worlds for a time, through no small effort of your own intuition and daring. You have been noticed, Hugh Reid."

Hugh was uncomfortably torn between an overflowing sense of self-worth to be so complimented by such a being, and hand-wringing anxiety as to what "being noticed" meant.

"I assume," Odin went on, "that the discovery of your true heritage, of your power in your world, of your family, might be perceived as a sufficient reward. Treat them well, and learn them well. Trying times are ahead, but the tools of victory are already yours. Fear not, and remember: I've got my eye on you."

Odin tossed his grey-bearded head back to unleash a hearty laugh, which the assembled host echoed dutifully.

Then, eight-legged Sleipnir reared and bounded away with the huntsmen hard on his heels. As the baying horns faded into the mist, the Nuggle gave the psychic equivalent of a polite silence-breaking cough.

<HUGH REID, PLEASE REMOVE THIS FIEND.>

Confused, Hugh looked down, only to see that the Hunt had left a hound behind. The small pup had its stubby fangs latched around the Nuggle's ankle and was idly chewing. Grey-green eyes peered up at Hugh from under chocolate eyespots in a black-furred face. Brown traced his lips in a joker's smile, and his brown-tipped paws were almost comically too big for his stubby legs. Dismounting from the Nuggle's damp back, Hugh crouched and offered open hands to the puppy. The young fiend released his hold of the Nuggle's salty ankle and pounced to the Warden, his thick black tail whirl-wagging.

<FASCINATING,> the Nuggle commented. When Hugh glanced up from petting velvety triangular ears, he confirmed from the waterhorse's furrowed brow the concern he thought he'd heard in its psychic voice.

<THIS IS NOT THE TIME FOR THE HUNT TO CROSS REALMS,> explained the Nuggle, <NOT FOR THREE SEASONS YET. THEY SEEM TO HAVE LEFT YOU THIS BEAST TO SAFEGUARD IN THE MEANTIME.>

"Beast?" Hugh crooned in the universal voice that is instinctively reserved for babies. "He's just a wee pup; what harm can he possibly do?"

Intelligence sparkled in those cunning little eyes.

Wide paws tucked together under his round belly; his eager gaze never left Hugh's face as he gathered himself. Curved fangs flashed as his stout maw opened to bark, and the concussive sound knocked Hugh back on his heels. Rather than produce a yip more suited to his size, the black-and-tan hound's voice was as loud as the vastness of the universe.

Odin's departing laugh rang in Hugh's ears as he stared, aghast, at the grinning pup and wondered just what he'd been dragged in to now.

First Edition

Copyright © 2019 Nicole R. Ordway

Edited by Jeanne L. Wilkins

Cover Aurora Imagery by Ann Dinsmore

HCS Publishing

www.hcspublishing.com

All rights reserved.

ISBN: 978-0-578-48504-1